THE ONE

FOUR FAE FOR THE PRINCESS
BOOK ONE

SADIE WATERS

For Jessie

CONTENTS

CHAPTER 1
THE PRINCESS IS THROWING A BALL

Maerilee

The dog treat trembles in my hand, faint pulses of magic swirling around it like threads of silver. I close my eyes, focusing on the barrier I'm trying to create. The energies stretch from my fingertips, encasing the treat in an invisible shield, or at least what I hope is an invisible shield. My breath slows as I concentrate, willing the magic to hold steady. A faint hum tickles the back of my mind. My magic is attempting to do what it's supposed to but deep down, I can feel how weak it is, how flimsy the barrier must be.

I open my eyes, my gaze flicking to my dog, Duchess, curled up in a ball on my bed. Her small body rises and falls softly as she sleeps, completely unaware of the challenge I'm facing.

The barrier needs to be perfect. If I can't even manage this, what hope do I have of fortifying the one protecting our kingdom?

"Just focus, Maerilee," I murmur to myself. My fingers flex, sending another ripple of energy through the shield. It looks solid enough, a faint shimmer around the treat.

Suddenly, Duchess stirs. I glance up as her nose twitches, nostrils flaring as she catches the scent of the treat. My heart sinks.

"No, no, no," I whisper, watching as Duchess's little black eyes blink open. She lifts her head, giving a lazy yawn before hopping off the bed. Her tiny paws pad across the floor as she heads straight for me, or rather, the treat in front of me.

"Stay back, Duchess," I warn softly, though I know it's useless. I have something she wants and she's determined to go after it.

Her nose pokes at the invisible barrier, her little pink tongue darting out to taste the air. I sit up straighter, holding my breath. This is the moment. If the barrier holds, Duchess won't be able to—

She walks right through it.

My jaw drops as she simply passes through the shimmering magic, the protective shield crumbling like dust. She doesn't even notice the weak flicker of power. Before I can react, she snatches the treat in her mouth, tail wagging furiously, and trots off proudly.

"Duchess!" I groan, collapsing onto the floor, defeated. She prances out of the room like she's just conquered a mighty foe, while I sit here, a mess of frustration and failure.

This is hopeless. I'll never be able to help strengthen the kingdom's barrier if I can't even master a small barrier spell for a dog treat.

As if on cue, someone knocks at my door. I sit up quickly, trying to compose myself, though I can still feel the sting of embarrassment heating my cheeks. The door opens slightly, and Akin steps into the room just as Duchess struts out, tail wagging with her prize.

"Good to see Duchess is well-fed," he comments with a grin, clearly amused at the scene. His dark eyes flick to me, concern immediately replacing the humor when he notices my posture, slumped on the floor.

"I was practicing," I mutter, sitting up straighter and brushing my hair out of my face. "It didn't exactly go as planned."

Akin steps fully into the room, closing the door behind him. He looks down at me with that familiar, steady gaze, the one that never seems to waver, even when everything around us is falling apart.

He's always so sure of himself, always so capable. I feel a pang of jealousy in my chest before I can push it down.

"You'll get it," he says, his voice low and reassuring. "But right now, your parents want to see you."

I nod, feeling a tight knot form in the pit of my stomach. "Now?"

"Now," he confirms with a solemn nod. "It sounded important."

Of course, it's important. Everything is important these days. I stand up, dusting off my gown, and catch a glimpse of myself in the mirror. My long whitish hair, tinged with lavender, is slightly tangled, and my silver eyes seem a little dimmer than usual. I smooth my hair down with a sigh and follow Akin out of the room.

As we walk through the palace halls, I can't help but glance at him from the corner of my eye. He walks with such purpose, his tall, broad frame radiating strength. I've known Akin my whole life, but there's always been this distance between us, one that feels more like a wall now than ever before. He's my bodyguard, yes, but sometimes it feels like something more. Or maybe it's just me.

We reach the doors to my parents' chamber, and Akin gives me a small nod before stepping back. I take a deep breath, preparing myself for whatever they're going to say. I push open the doors and step into the familiar warmth of the room.

My mother, Queen Kimalissa, sits near the window, looking out over the kingdom. The soft light filtering in through the glass highlights the weariness in her face. Every day, the weight of the kingdom's failing barrier seems to press harder on her, making her look more and more fragile. It breaks my heart to see her like this.

My father, King Fratino, stands beside her, his tall frame tense, though he manages to offer me a small smile as I enter. His moon-touched skin glows faintly, a reminder of the power he holds. It's a power that comes so naturally to him, unlike me. I don't even know if I have a 'One,' let alone the ability to do what's needed for our kingdom.

"Maerilee," my mother says, turning to face me with an expression that immediately makes my stomach drop. It's the look she gives when she's about to ask something of me that I'm not going to like.

"Mother, Father," I greet them with a small curtsy, trying to keep my voice steady.

"We've been talking," my father begins, glancing at my mother before continuing. "Given the current state of things, we've decided it's time to take more decisive action in finding your One."

I blink, anxiety rippling through me. "Decisive action?"

My mother sighs, walking toward me with a grace that belies her exhaustion. "We've sent out invitations to the surrounding kingdoms," she says softly. "To all eligible noblemen."

My heart skips a beat, a mix of anger and embarrassment flaring up inside me. "Eligible for what?"

"For you," my father says bluntly, his voice firm. "We're hosting a month-long ball, Maerilee. In the hopes of fostering peace, yes, but mainly to help you find your One."

The words hang in the air between us, and for a moment, I can't speak. They've invited noblemen, strangers from rival kingdoms, to come here and parade themselves around, all in the hope that one of them might be my One? I feel a surge of frustration rising inside me, but I bite my tongue.

I know why they're doing this. I know how important it is but it still stings. Once again, I'm faced with my own failures.

"I see," I say, my voice tighter than I intended.

"Maerilee, we understand how difficult this must be for you," my mother says, her eyes pleading. "But the barrier is weakening every day, and we don't have much time. If you find your One, if you can unlock the power that comes with it, you can help restore it."

I swallow hard, the weight of her words pressing down on me. I know she's right. The barrier is crumbling, and with it, our kingdom's protection. I can see it in the way my mother's once-vibrant magic has dimmed, the way her strength seems to slip away a little more each day. If I don't do something, if I don't find my One, Altinna could fall to invasion.

Still, that doesn't make it any easier to hear.

"I understand," I finally say, my voice quiet but steady. "I'll do whatever is necessary."

My mother's expression softens, relief flickering in her eyes. "Thank you, Maerilee. I know this isn't easy."

"No, it's not," I admit, looking between her and my father. "But if this is what's needed, I'll attend the ball. I'll meet these noblemen. I'll try to find my One."

As the words leave my mouth, a strange mix of dread and determination settles over me. I've spent so long searching, waiting for some sign that I even have a One. But what if this ball changes nothing? What if none of these men are the one I'm supposed to bond with?

What if I'm destined to fail?

But I push those thoughts aside, forcing myself to focus on the task ahead. I have to try for Altinna.

I'll find my One. I have to.

My powers depend on it. My future depends on it. When I find my One, I'll have full access to the powers I innately possess. After our binding ceremony, my wings will come in, and I'll be complete, whole. It's what I've been waiting for my whole life.

As I turn to leave the room, my mother's voice stops me.

"Maerilee," she says softly. "No matter what happens, we're proud of you."

I nod, unable to trust myself to speak. Akin is waiting just outside, his expression unreadable as he watches me approach. He doesn't ask what happened. He doesn't need to. He already knows.

"Let's go," I say quietly, embarrassment flooding me. "I'd very much like to be alone now."

CHAPTER 2
THE GRAND ENTRANCE

Maerilee

I stand in front of the mirror, assessing my reflection. The lavender gown clings perfectly to my frame, the soft fabric shimmering with every movement. It's a beautiful dress, hand-sewn with threads of silver that match the pale glow of my hair, but all I can think about is how much I wish I didn't have to wear it.

I'm not looking forward to this grand spectacle to parade me around in front of foreign nobles, all in the hopes of finding my One. The thought alone makes me clench my fists, the material of my skirt crinkling under my hands. I smooth it out with a shaky breath.

I can do this. I have to do this.

The weight of expectation is heavy on my shoulders as I turn away from the mirror, heading toward the door where Akin waits. He's dressed in formal attire, his expression as unreadable as ever.

"Are you ready?" he asks.

I nod, though my heart is pounding in my chest. "As ready as I'll ever be."

He offers a slight smile but doesn't say anything more. He guides me through the palace corridors, the sound of our footsteps echoing off the marble floors. My palms are slick with nervousness, and I try to wipe them discreetly on my gown, but Akin notices.

"You look beautiful," he assures me, his voice low but steady.

I glance at him, surprised by the compliment. He rarely says things like that.

"Thank you," I whisper, too stunned to say much else.

We reach the grand staircase leading down to the ballroom, and my stomach flips. The doors below are already open, and I can hear the distant murmur of voices, the music, the clinking of glasses. The grand chandelier is glowing brightly, casting light over the elegantly dressed fae who have gathered from every corner of Haebradia. This is it.

Akin gives me one last look. "I'll be nearby if you need me."

I nod, swallowing hard as I take my place at the top of the staircase. The herald stands beside me, poised and ready to announce my arrival. His deep voice booms across the ballroom, cutting through the noise below.

"Her Highness, Princess Maerilee of Altinna."

As if on cue, every head turns toward me. The room goes quiet, the murmurs dying down into a hush as I take my first step down the staircase. My gown trails softly behind me, the lavender fabric catching the light, making me feel ethereal.

All eyes are on me, noblemen and women from every kingdom, fae of every type and color. I can see the glittering wings of the Sylvan fae, who get their wings whether they're bound or not, the horns of the Briarwood folk, the towering forms of the Stonekin. The tension in the room is palpable, a mix of curiosity and expectation as they watch me descend. They all know tonight's purpose. They're all wondering if I'll find my One tonight.

The pressure is suffocating.

As I reach the bottom step, I brace myself for a feeling. I've been told that when I meet my One, I'll feel it immediately. My mother always spoke of a pull, a connection so strong that it's undeniable.

She felt it the moment she laid eyes on my father. She said it was like a magnetic force, drawing them together in an instant.

So as I step into the ballroom and the crowd parts slightly, I wait for that feeling. I scan the faces in the room, searching for a spark, a sign that one of them is him.

But nothing happens.

There's no rush of energy, no magnetic pull. Just the overwhelming sense of being watched by hundreds of strangers, each one silently judging me. I can feel the weight of their gazes, some curious, others assessing. I try to smile, to maintain the composure that's expected of me, but inside, a gnawing sense of panic begins to build.

What if none of them are him? What if I'm destined to be a powerless, flightless fae for the rest of my life?

The ballroom is grand, the walls lined with gold filigree, and the chandeliers overhead cast a warm, golden glow over everything. Musicians play softly in the corner, the delicate notes of a harp weaving through the air. Fae of every creed and color mingle, their fine clothes shimmering as they move.

I feel out of place among them, like a piece of a puzzle that doesn't quite fit. My magic flickers weakly inside me, a constant reminder that I'm not like them. Not yet.

Akin

I stand at the edge of the ballroom, blending into the shadows cast by the ornate pillars. My eyes never leave Maerilee, though I make sure to stay unobtrusive, just as I always do. I'm not meant to be noticed tonight. No one is supposed to see me here. This is her night, not mine.

She looks radiant, as always, in her lavender gown. The way the fabric catches the light and shimmers as she moves is enough to steal anyone's breath. But it's not the gown or the way her hair gleams under the chandeliers that holds my attention. It's *her*.

She's nervous as she scans the crowd, and from where I stand, I can see the exact moment when that nervousness deepens into something darker. She's searching for her One. I know it. I've been dreading this moment since the day her parents announced the ball.

I let out a breath I hadn't realized I was holding when I see the look of consternation on her face. She's scanning the crowd, hoping, waiting for the spark, the connection her mother always talks about. But it's not there. Not yet.

I should feel anxious for her, but all I feel is relief.

Relief that she hasn't found him. That she hasn't locked eyes with some stranger across the room and felt that pull, that undeniable bond that will tie her to another for the rest of her life. That will tie her to someone who isn't me.

The second I acknowledge that, I'm angry at myself for it.

I know better. I've always known better. Maerilee finding her One is what's best for Altinna. The kingdom needs her at her full power, and she can't manifest it alone. Her One, whoever he is, will be the key to unlocking that. And I want that for her. I want the kingdom to be safe, to thrive. I want Maerilee to have the strength she needs to protect the kingdom.

But wanting that means losing her. And I don't know how to reconcile the two. She'll fly off with some foreign prince or dignitary, and I'll be reassigned, likely. Only the royals in our kingdom are granted the gift of flight. I'll be no good to her then.

I've been by Maerilee's side for as long as I can remember. I remember when she was just a little girl, full of wild energy, running barefoot through the palace gardens while I tried to keep up with her. She was always faster than me back then, laughing over her shoulder as I chased her through the roses and up the old oak tree that grew near the palace gates.

We weren't supposed to climb that tree, of course. It was forbidden, but that didn't stop her. It never stopped her.

One day, she fell from one of the branches, scraping her knee on the way down. She was crying, sitting in the dirt with her dress torn, and I rushed over to her, panicked. I was ready to run for help, but she grabbed my arm and pulled me down next to her.

"I'm okay," she said, through tears and hiccups. "It doesn't even hurt that bad."

She wiped at her face furiously, and I could see the stubborn pride in her even then. She hated crying. Hated showing weakness. I sat with her, unsure of what to do, and then she grabbed my hand.

"You can't tell anyone, okay? Promise."

I promised. Of course, I promised. I would've promised her anything.

From that day forward, it was always Maerilee and me. Somewhere along the way, things shifted. She stopped being just the princess I was sworn to protect, and she became something more.

I don't know when it happened. Maybe it was gradual, or maybe it was all at once. But one day, I looked at her, and she wasn't just the girl with scraped knees and a fierce determination to prove herself. She was everything. And I realized, painfully, that I loved her.

It's a love I know I can never have, not the way I want. She's the future queen of Altinna, and her destiny is tied to another. The entire kingdom depends on her finding her One, on the bond that will give her the strength to maintain the magical barrier that keeps us all safe.

I understand that. I've accepted it. But that doesn't stop my heart from breaking a little more every time I'm near her.

And now, watching her in this ballroom, knowing what's at stake, I feel like I'm being torn in two. Part of me wants her to find him, to feel that connection and finally be at peace with her powers, with her future. But the selfish part of me hopes she never does.

CHAPTER 3
A SWING AND A MISS

Maerilee

The ballroom swirls with color and light, the soft hum of conversation mingling with the music that drifts through the air. I try to keep a pleasant expression on my face, to hide the gnawing frustration that's slowly taking root inside me. My mother told me that she felt it instantly, that deep, magical pull when she found my father. One glance, one meeting of the eyes, and she knew. It was that simple. That certain.

But I've been circling this room for what feels like an eternity, and I haven't felt even the faintest hint of it.

I smile and nod at yet another nobleman, some duke's son whose name I can't even remember now. He bows, his eyes bright with interest, but when our gazes meet—nothing. No spark, no sense of recognition, just an awkward silence before he steps away, clearly hoping to find an engaging conversation.

I sigh, trying not to let the disappointment show. I move on, my eyes scanning the room, searching the faces of every man I pass. Maybe I've missed him. Maybe I haven't given it enough time. Surely, I'll feel something soon. Won't I?

The air is thick with expectation, as if everyone here is waiting for something to happen. I'm waiting, too. But as the evening wears on, the weight of it grows heavier, pressing down on me until I can barely breathe.

I take a deep, steadying breath and let my gaze wander again. That's when I see a young prince leaning casually against a wall near one of the alcoves. His name escapes me, but I recognize him as the second son of the king and queen of Oceana. His dark hair falls over his forehead, and there's an easy confidence in the way he stands, like he's completely unbothered by the pomp and ceremony around him. He's not fawning over anyone, not seeking attention like so many of the others. He's just watching.

I hesitate for a moment, wondering if I should go over to him. He intrigues me, not like the other noblemen who keep trying to prove themselves to me. He's quiet, more reserved, but there's something in his eyes that makes me think he sees more than he lets on.

I take a step in his direction, but before I can reach him, a figure steps into my path.

"Princess Maerilee," the man says, his voice slick with charm. His smile is wide, too wide, and there's a gleam in his eye that immediately puts me on edge. He bows with exaggerated flourish, his golden hair catching the light as he rises. "Surely you weren't about to waste your time with my younger brother, Brook, were you?"

I recognize him immediately as River, the Crown Prince of Oceana. "I wasn't—"

"Because," he interrupts smoothly, stepping closer, "I can assure you, Princess, he's not what you need. *I* am what you need."

I frown, taken aback by his arrogance. "Excuse me?"

He smirks, clearly mistaking my confusion for interest. "Brook is fine if you want someone to waste time with, but let's be honest, Maerilee. You're the future queen of Altinna. You need someone of higher standing. Someone with power. Someone who can help you rule."

He takes another step toward me, his hand reaching out to brush lightly against the small of my back. I resist the urge to pull away, keeping my expression neutral.

"And let me guess," I say, my voice dry. "You think that someone is you."

He grins, not catching the sarcasm. "Of course it is. I'm a Crown Prince, after all. My kingdom is strong, prosperous, and I have the experience you need. Together, we'd be unstoppable."

I stare at him, barely able to believe his audacity. He's still talking, now listing his various achievements, all while managing to subtly imply that I'm not nearly as competent as I should be. That without him, I'll probably fail.

"And honestly," he adds with a wink, "it's not like you're going to find anyone better here. I'm clearly the best choice for you."

I feel my temper flare, but I force myself to stay calm. I've dealt with men like River before. He's entitled, arrogant, and thinks the world should bend to his will just because he's been handed power. I'm not about to let him think he can speak to me like that.

I smile, sweetly. "River," I say, keeping my tone light, "while I appreciate your... *confidence*, let me make one thing very clear."

He leans in, clearly expecting some sort of praise. "Yes?"

"I would sooner take my chances with a rock than tie myself to someone as utterly insufferable as you."

His smile falters. "What?"

I step past him, my smile never wavering. "I'm sure your kingdom is doing just fine, but I'd rather not spend another moment listening to you talk about yourself. Good evening."

I don't wait for his response, simply heading straight for Brook.

RIVER

I watch Maerilee walk away, my eyes narrowed as she disappears into the crowd, headed straight for my brother. A mixture of disbelief and amusement stirs in my chest. Did she really just brush me off like that? Most girls would have been swooning by now, falling over themselves for just a sliver of my attention. But Maerilee didn't even blink. She shut me down with the sort of icy composure I've only seen in queens.

That was unexpected.

Who is she to dismiss me like I'm just another forgettable suitor? Yet beneath the insult, there's a flicker of something else. Admiration, maybe. Most of the women I've encountered are so busy batting their eyelashes and hanging on my every word that they don't even realize when I'm undermining them. It's almost too easy, too predictable. They lap up the compliments, never noticing the jabs I slip in between.

But she saw right through me. And she didn't just call me out on it—she *walked away* like I was barely worth her time.

Impressive.

I smirk to myself, folding my arms as I lean back against one of the marble pillars, watching her with a newfound interest. She's making her way to Brook now, poor fool. I can't help but chuckle under my breath. It's only a matter of time before she realizes what a mistake that is. My brother might seem intriguing to someone like her, all brooding and quiet, standing in the shadows like he's too deep for the rest of us, but I know better. Brook isn't the knight in shining armor she's hoping for. He's just another disappointment waiting to happen.

Still, I'll give her credit. She's a lot sharper than I expected.

I glance around the ballroom, the glittering crowd of fae and noblemen swirling like a sea of colors and wealth. The music plays on, and the hum of conversation fills the air. Everyone here has an agenda. It's all a game, really. And I've always been good at games.

Maerilee is a different kind of player, though. She doesn't seem like the type to be easily manipulated, which makes her all the more interesting. Shame she's not my One. I suppose I'd actually enjoy matching wits with her, at least for a time.

My gaze drifts to Brook again, and I shake my head. This is

going to be a disaster. The moment she gets close to him, she'll realize he's nothing special. He might have the looks, but that's about it. He's too serious, too introspective for a girl like her. She needs someone who can keep up with her, challenge her. Someone like me.

I feel a flicker of irritation as I watch her laugh at something he says, but I quickly push it aside. No sense in getting worked up over this. If she wants to waste her time with him, that's her mistake. I'll be here when she realizes her error. The kingdom will need someone like me eventually, whether she sees it now or not.

In Oceana, we don't even need wings to fly. We can harness the power of our water magic to travel. And unlike the primitive, matriarchal society of Altinna, we don't have to wait to find our "One" for our powers to manifest. Even unbound, I'm stronger than Maerilee ever could be. Certainly stronger than Brook. There's nothing he can offer her that I can't give 100 times over.

I let my eyes wander across the ballroom, scanning the crowd with a more practical intent. If Maerilee isn't interested, there's no reason to waste the rest of the evening. There are plenty of other women here who would be more than happy to entertain me for the night. After all, the ball is only the beginning of the festivities. There's always an after-party, always rooms tucked away in some dark corridor where we can slip away unnoticed.

My gaze lands on a serving maid, her auburn hair catching the candlelight as she moves gracefully through the crowd, carrying a tray of wine goblets. She's slender, with wide, innocent eyes and a soft smile. The kind of girl who looks up at you with wonder, who believes every compliment you feed her. I imagine how easy it would be to pull her aside, whisper a few sweet nothings in her ear, and have her melting into my arms before the night is over.

Yes. She'll do.

I watch her for a moment, tracking her movements as she weaves in and out of the guests, completely unaware that she's already been chosen. There's something satisfying about knowing I can have her with just a few words. It's all a game, really. And I always win.

But first, I'll finish watching this little train wreck with Maerilee and Brook. It's not often I get to witness my brother make a fool of himself in real-time, and I'd hate to miss the show. I cross my arms over my chest, settling in for what's sure to be a catastrophe.

CHAPTER 4

QUIET CONVERSATIONS

Maerilee

I move toward Brook, a smile on my lips as I approach. The grand ballroom is still buzzing with laughter and conversation, but all of that fades into the background as I focus on him. He's leaning against a wall, arms crossed, his expression detached, almost like he's observing everything from a distance, like he's in the room but not really part of it.

He glances up as I approach, his eyes meeting mine for a brief moment before darting to either side, as if to check if I'm actually heading toward him. The surprise in his gaze is subtle, but it's there. He wasn't expecting this. I can't help but find it a little amusing. Did he really think I wouldn't notice him, standing off to the side like that?

"Brook," I say, my voice light, as though we're simply old friends catching up. "You're hiding over here like you don't want to be found."

I stop a few steps in front of him, my smile widening just a fraction. He straightens, uncrossing his arms, but he still looks a bit stiff, like he's not sure what to do with himself. I get the sense he's uncomfortable, and I wonder why. He doesn't strike me as the type to get flustered, but there's something about his posture that feels uneasy.

He gives me a nod, but it's awkward, almost reluctant. "I'm not hiding," he says, his voice low and measured, as if he's carefully choosing his words. "Just observing."

I raise an eyebrow, tilting my head slightly. "And what have you observed so far?"

Brook shifts his weight from one foot to the other, his gaze flicking away from mine for a moment before returning. "That you're doing a lot of circulating."

I laugh softly. "Guilty as charged. I suppose I'm doing what's expected of me."

He doesn't respond right away, and I take a step closer, lowering my voice a little. "I hope I'm not interrupting your observation. I thought you might want some company."

Brook glances at me, and for the briefest moment, I think I see something flicker in his eyes. It's warm, like he appreciates the gesture, but it's gone as quickly as it appeared. He shrugs slightly, but his shoulders remain tense. "It's fine. You're not interrupting."

I search his face, trying to figure out what's going on in his mind. His responses are clipped, careful, like he's trying to keep some part of himself hidden.

I wonder if it's the pressure of the evening getting to him. The ball, the expectations, the constant scrutiny from everyone around us. It's overwhelming enough for me, and I'm used to this kind of thing. Maybe Brook just isn't comfortable in these kinds of settings. Maybe he's nervous, and that thought makes me soften my approach a little.

"I'm not a big fan of all this either," I say, gesturing vaguely to the ballroom, the pomp and circumstance of it all. "But it's what we have to do, right? Part of the duty of being who we are."

He glances at me again, and this time, there's a hint of understanding in his expression. "I guess so," he mutters.

There's a moment of silence between us, and I can't help but feel a little disheartened. I was hoping for something more. I didn't expect fireworks, but I thought maybe I'd feel *something* stronger when I looked at Brook.

Yet again, I feel nothing.

Well, not *nothing*. I do feel something, a pull, maybe—a sense that Brook is important in some way. But it's not the all-consuming certainty I was hoping for. It's not the *One* feeling. And as much as I try to shake it off, the disappointment is there, lingering at the back of my mind.

Still, I can't let Brook see how discouraged I am. I keep smiling, determined to make the most of this moment, or at least have a real conversation with him.

"You seem a little tense," I say, keeping my tone light. "Are you okay?"

He hesitates, his gaze shifting to the floor for a second before meeting mine again.

"I'm fine," he responds, though the tightness in his voice suggests otherwise. "This is just a little overwhelming."

I nod, understanding.

"It's a lot, isn't it?" I breathe out. "All these people, all this pressure"

He doesn't answer right away, but I can see his posture relax, like he appreciates the acknowledgment. I take another step closer, lowering my voice so it's just the two of us in this moment.

"You don't have to pretend with me, you know. I feel it too. Every eye is on me tonight, everyone just waiting for me to either find my One or fail. It's exhausting."

Brook glances at me, and this time, there's something softer in his gaze. He looks like he's on the verge of saying something, but then he stops, his jaw tightening as if he's holding himself back.

BROOK

Maerilee is talking to me.

I can't quite wrap my head around it. Her voice is soft, sure, and when she speaks, it's like every word is carried on a gentle breeze, light but impossible to ignore. I glance around the grand ballroom, half-expecting to see someone watching with a smug grin on their face, like this is some elaborate joke. Someone dared her, surely, to talk to the lesser prince, the one who lurks in the shadows while the rest of the court dances in the light.

But there's no one else. No one behind her giggling, no secret looks being exchanged across the room. It's just her. Maerilee, the princess of Altinna, with her long whitish hair that shimmers with lavender in the candlelight and those silver eyes that are looking straight at me, like I matter.

"So, Brook," she says, her voice cutting through the noise of the ball, "what do you think of Altinna?"

I blink, thrown by the question. What do I think of Altinna? What kind of question is that? I've barely seen the place. We're only here for the ball, and it hasn't left much time for forming opinions.

I clear my throat, trying to come up with something that sounds halfway intelligent.

"It's beautiful," I manage, which feels both true and terribly inadequate. "The architecture especially. The way the palace blends into the landscape. It's like it's a part of the mountains."

She smiles, and for a moment, I'm stunned by how genuine it looks. Not the practiced, polite smile royalty tends to wear at these events, but something warmer.

"That's what I think, too," she answers with excitement. "I love that about the palace. It's like the stones themselves are alive, holding up the walls, protecting us." She pauses, looking a little wistful. "They've been doing that for a long time."

Her words hang in the air, and I get the sense she's talking about more than just the stones. There's a heaviness behind her eyes that I hadn't noticed before, a weight of responsibility that feels far too great for someone as young as she is. It's strange. She's a princess, destined to rule, yet in this moment, she seems lonely.

I'm not used to this, to conversations like this. People don't talk to me. Not like this. Not as if what I think matters. My brother, River, is usually the one who gets all the attention. He's the handsome one, the charismatic one. He's also arrogant as hell. I glance over at him now, and sure enough, he's in his element, flirting with one of the Altinnaen noblewomen, making her laugh with whatever charming nonsense he's spouting. I don't know how he does it.

When I look back at Maerilee, she's still watching me, her eyes curious.

We start talking about art, my favorite subject, and for the first time in what feels like forever, I don't feel awkward or out of place. Maerilee listens to everything I say, really listens, and asks questions that show she's genuinely interested. It's not just polite small talk. She's engaged, thoughtful, and kind.

Then I notice, out of the corner of my eye, that River has been watching us. At first, I think it's just because he's bored, but then I see the tightness in his jaw, the way his eyes narrow every time I make Maerilee laugh.

Is he jealous?

The thought is almost laughable. River, the golden prince, jealous of me, the shadow. It doesn't make sense. But I can see it in his expression, the frustration, the simmering anger. He can't stand that I'm talking to her, that she's paying attention to me and not him.

I try to ignore it, focusing instead on Maerilee's next question about water magic and how it can be used to enhance art. I'm halfway through explaining a technique I've been working on when I see it.

A thin layer of ice forms on the floor just behind a servant who's carrying a tray of spring wine.

River.

I don't know if he meant it as a prank or if he's just lashing out, but it's clear what's about to happen. The servant steps onto the ice, his feet slipping out from under him. The tray flies into the air, and an entire bottle's worth of wine heads straight for Maerilee.

Time slows. Without thinking, I reach out with my magic, feeling the water in the wine, the way it moves through the air. I focus, guiding it, redirecting it. The wine curves away from Maerilee at the last second, swirling through the air like a ribbon.

And then it dumps itself over River's head.

CHAPTER 5
DISASTER NOT AVERTED

Maerilee

The moment the wine splashes over River, soaking him head to toe in red, I almost can't stop the grin that pulls at my lips. I catch myself before it fully forms, pressing my hand to my mouth in an attempt to look concerned. But inside, I'm more than a little pleased.

River has spent the entire evening trying to undermine Brook, I can see that clearly. There's an air about him, a kind of casual cruelty, like everything he touches should bend to his will. I'm not certain, but I suspect that the spill was his fault in the first place. Still, seeing him get a taste of his own mischief, even if it's accidental, feels oddly satisfying.

Brook stands there beside me, looking slightly startled by what he's done, yet doesn't seem the least bit guilty. If anything, he seems almost surprised it worked out the way it did.

I turn to him, allowing my smile to show now that I know River can't see me.

"That was impressive," I say, my voice soft but sincere. "Thank you for saving my dress. Your control over your water magic is remarkable."

Brook's eyes widen slightly, as though he can't quite believe I'm complimenting him.

"It was nothing," he mutters, glancing down at the floor, as though unsure of what to do with praise. "I just didn't want you to get soaked."

"Well, I'm grateful," I continue, my tone genuine.

He shifts on his feet, clearly uncomfortable with the attention, but I can see a small flicker of pride in his eyes. It's subtle, but it's there.

Before I can say anything else, though, I catch sight of movement across the room. My stomach tightens as I watch the king and queen of Oceana, his parents, marching toward us with River trailing behind, his face a thunderstorm of anger and humiliation. There's no way this is going to end well.

I feel a protective instinct rise within me, a sudden need to shield Brook from whatever is about to happen. He doesn't deserve this. But before I can figure out how to intervene, they're already upon us.

"Brook!" King Alastair's voice cuts through the air like a whip, cold and commanding. His eyes, hard as ice, lock onto his youngest son. "What is the meaning of this?"

Brook doesn't say a word. He stands there, silent, his head slightly bowed, refusing to meet his father's gaze. I can feel the tension radiating from him, the weight of years of unspoken grievances and slights pressing down on him.

Queen Lyria's face is a mask of disdain as she looks Brook up and down, her lips curled in disapproval. "How could you be so careless?" she demands, her voice sharp. "This is beyond irresponsible, Brook."

River, of course, steps forward, dripping wine but looking entirely smug, as if this whole incident is somehow Brook's fault and not his own.

"Typical," he mutters, loud enough for everyone to hear. "Always causing trouble. He couldn't even make it through one evening without embarrassing us."

I grit my teeth, feeling a surge of anger on Brook's behalf. I want to say something, anything to defend him, but I'm not sure it's my place. These are his parents, after all. They outrank me here, even if I am the heir to Altinna.

But Brook doesn't even try to defend himself. He stands there, taking the berating in silence, his shoulders slightly hunched as though he's been through this a thousand times before. Maybe he has.

I can't let this go on.

"Actually," I interject, stepping forward so that I'm standing next to Brook, "it was an accident. The servant slipped on some ice, and Brook used his magic to keep the wine from spilling on me." I glance pointedly at River, though I don't say anything else. It's enough that he knows I'm aware.

King Alastair's eyes flicker to me, but his expression remains hard, unmoved.

"An accident?" he repeats, his voice cold. "I find that hard to believe."

"It's true," I insist, keeping my voice steady. "And Brook's quick thinking saved me from being drenched in wine. He deserves to be thanked, not reprimanded."

Queen Lyria's gaze shifts to me now, her expression softening just a fraction, but only because I'm a princess, no doubt. "Your Highness, while we appreciate your defense of Brook, this kind of recklessness is unacceptable."

"Recklessness?" I ask, my brow furrowing. "What's reckless about using one's magic to help others? He did nothing wrong. If anything, he prevented a larger mess from happening."

I can feel Brook tense beside me, like he's bracing for whatever backlash might come next. He's still silent, still not defending himself, and I wonder how long he's been conditioned to simply take whatever harsh words are thrown his way.

River, however, can't help but chime in again, his voice dripping with false innocence. "Perhaps if Brook focused more on his responsibilities and less on showing off, things like this wouldn't happen."

I shoot River a glare, and for a brief moment, I wish I had some magic that could put him in his place. But I don't. All I have are my words, and I intend to use them.

"Showing off?" I repeat, incredulous. "Brook wasn't showing off. He was helping. If that's what you consider showing off, then maybe you should reconsider what you define as 'responsibility,' River."

River opens his mouth to retort, but King Alastair raises a hand, silencing him. "Enough," he says, his voice heavy with finality. He turns his cold gaze back to Brook, and for a moment, I think he might say something more—something cruel, perhaps—but instead, he just sighs, a long, disappointed sound. "You've caused enough trouble for one night, Brook. We'll discuss this later."

Just as I'm about to try again, I catch sight of my mother and father making their way toward us. I can tell by the looks on their faces that they've come to smooth things over, as they always do. Mother walks with the calm grace of someone who's used to handling problems with a mere flick of her wrist. Father follows close behind, his expression stern but composed.

"Your Highness," my mother says, addressing me but clearly speaking for the benefit of those around us, "we deeply apologize for the servant's clumsiness. Such accidents are regrettable, and we'll make sure it's dealt with."

I nod, though the apology feels hollow. This wasn't the servant's fault, and I know it. But before I can respond, I feel a presence beside me, and I turn to see Akin. His dark eyes meet mine, and I can see the flicker of something unsaid in his gaze.

He leans in close, his voice low but insistent.

"Maerilee, I saw what happened. It wasn't an accident." His words send a chill down my spine, and I can feel my heart start to race. "Prince River formed a patch of ice under the servant, causing him to slip. He did it on purpose. I imagine he was jealous that you were talking so fondly with his brother."

I blink, my mind reeling. Of course, I'd suspected River was involved, but hearing it confirmed like this makes my blood boil. The audacity of him! His childish, mean-spirited prank that nearly ruined the evening, and then he had the gall to stand there and act like Brook was to blame. The anger builds inside me, a fire I can't suppress any longer.

I snap.

"River!" I shout, my voice rising over the voices of our parents, who are still discussing what happened. All eyes turn in my direction, waiting for what I'm going to say next. My pulse is pounding in my ears, but I don't care. "You're nothing but a man-child who can't even own up to his own misdeeds!"

A hush falls over the assembled crowd, and for a moment, it feels like the entire room has frozen in place. River looks like he's been struck. His face flushes red with both embarrassment and anger, and his eyes narrow in my direction.

His parents are clearly shocked. Queen Lyria's mouth falls open in disbelief, while King Alastair's face hardens, his eyes blazing with fury.

"River," he growls, his voice cold and commanding, "what does she mean by this?"

River hesitates, his gaze flickering between me, his parents, and the crowd that's now hanging on every word. For a moment, I think he's going to deny it, to lie to everyone but then his shoulders slump, and I see the guilt in his eyes. He knows he's been caught.

"It was just a joke," he mutters, his voice barely audible. "I didn't think it would—"

"How dare you embarrass us like this?" Queen Lyria hisses, her face contorted with rage. "In front of the entire court! I cannot believe you would be so irresponsible!"

King Alastair shakes his head, his disappointment evident. "This is disgraceful, River. We expected better from you."

I stand there, watching as River shrinks under the weight of his parents' scolding, but something about the scene feels wrong. It's not enough. Yes, they're furious at him for embarrassing them, for causing trouble at a royal event, but they haven't said a word about Brook. Not once have they acknowledged that their other son, the one who had to deal with River's cruelty, deserves an apology. And that only makes me angrier.

I open my mouth to point this out, to say exactly what I'm thinking, but before the words can leave my lips, I feel a hand on my arm. My mother's hand.

"Maerilee," she demands softly but firmly. "You've done enough. Stay out of it."

CHAPTER 6
NO REST FOR THE WEARY

Maerilee

The rest of the ball seems to drag on forever. My earlier outburst and the whole ordeal with River leaves a sour taste in my mouth, and despite my best efforts to shake it off, I remain testy for the remainder of the evening. The Oceanans have excused themselves for the night, with King Alastair and Queen Lyria offering a brief, tight-lipped promise of a formal apology tomorrow. I can still see River's embarrassed, red face in my mind, though the satisfaction I initially felt at calling him out has long since faded. Now, I just want the night to end.

None of the other guests spark even the slightest interest in me. They all blend into one monotonous sea of faces, false pleasantries, and meaningless small talk. I try to keep up appearances, but my thoughts keep drifting elsewhere, particularly to Brook and Akin. Of all the people I've met in my life—nobles, commoners, visiting dignitaries—the only ones I've ever felt even a faint connection to have been those two. There's something about Brook's quiet, steady presence that draws me in, even when he's being overshadowed by his brother. And then, of course, there's Akin. He's been at my side for as long as I can remember, a steady presence I could always rely on. His loyalty and humor have made him a trustworthy companion, and I can't imagine my life without him.

On the opposite end of the desire spectrum, there's River. A faint shiver of disgust runs down my spine at the thought of him. I did feel a faint sliver of something when he was around, but it wasn't attraction. No, it was something much closer to revulsion, if I'm being honest. The way he carries himself, always seeking attention, always trying to one-up everyone in the room is exhausting. I can't help but wonder if people only tolerate him because he's the Crown Prince. Either way, I'm certain River isn't my One.

And if it's not River, then it's certainly not anyone else in this room. As I glance around, I can tell with absolute certainty that none of the other ball-goers have what I'm looking for. I've tried to remain open, patient, even hopeful, but the tug I expect to feel when I meet my One just isn't there. My time to find him is growing shorter as the barrier around our kingdom grows weaker every day. A nagging sense of urgency rises within me, the ever-present anxiety that I need to find my One soon, before it's too late.

I decide I've had enough. There's no point in staying if I'm not enjoying myself, and I'm fairly certain that my One isn't here tonight. I'll excuse myself early, return to my chambers, and hopefully get some rest. Maybe tomorrow will bring clarity, or at least a reprieve from this endless search.

Just as I'm about to slip away, though, I feel a presence beside me. I turn, and there stands Direken, Crown Prince of Ambrosia, a confident smirk on his face as he bows slightly. He's impeccably dressed, his dark hair slicked back, and he carries himself with a kind of self-importance that immediately sets me on edge.

"Princess Maerilee," he says smoothly, his voice oozing with charm. "Would you do me the honor of sharing a dance before you retire for the evening?"

His boldness catches me off guard, but I quickly recover, reminding myself to remain polite. I know within a second that this man is definitely not my One. Still, I can't very well refuse without causing a scene, and I've had enough drama for one evening.

I smile tightly, giving a small nod.

"Of course, Prince Direken," I answer demurely. "One dance."

He leads me onto the dance floor, and the music swells around us. As we begin to move, I can't help but feel a slight twinge of discomfort. Direken is charming in his own way, sure, but there's something about him that makes me feel unsettled around him. Perhaps it's the way he talks, always with an air of superiority, as if he's trying to impress me with every word. Or maybe it's the way he looks at me, like I'm some prize to be won, rather than a person he's genuinely interested in.

"You look stunning tonight," Direken says, his voice low as we move in time with the music. "I must say, I've been looking forward to this dance all evening."

I force another smile.

"Thank you," I reply, though my heart isn't in it. My mind is elsewhere, already counting the minutes until I can excuse myself and leave this ball behind.

Direken continues to talk, though I can't help but tune him out. He drones on about his family's wealth, his accomplishments, the grand estates they own, all the things I'm sure I'm supposed to be impressed by. Yet all I feel is a growing sense of irritation. It's as if he's more interested in hearing himself speak than in genuinely engaging with me.

Despite his efforts, this dance is nothing more to me than a formality, an obligation I must fulfill before I can finally leave. And the more Direken talks, the more tired I feel. It's not just physical exhaustion, though the evening has certainly worn on me. It's a deeper kind of weariness, the kind that comes from constantly searching, constantly hoping, and never quite finding what you're looking for.

By the time the dance ends, I'm more than ready to be done with it. I step back, offering a polite curtsy.

"Thank you for the dance, Prince Direken," I say, keeping my voice steady and formal.

"The pleasure was all mine, Princess," he replies, though I can tell he's disappointed that the dance is over. He probably thought he could charm me, sweep me off my feet with his grandiose tales and smooth words. But it didn't work.

With the dance over, I finally allow myself to feel the full weight of my exhaustion. I don't need to pretend anymore. There's no more need to put on a smile or engage in polite conversation. I truly am tired, and I'm more than ready to retire for the evening.

"I believe I'll take my leave now," I say, glancing around the ballroom one last time. The music continues, couples twirling on the dance floor, their laughter and conversation filling the space. But I'm done. There's nothing left here for me tonight.

Direken bows once more.

"I hope you'll consider another dance next time, Your Highness."

I nod politely, though I know full well there won't be a next time. As I turn to leave, I feel a sense of relief wash over me. I can finally slip away from the noise, the crowd, the endless expectations.

As I make my way toward the exit, I catch a glimpse of Brook standing near the edge of the ballroom. He's watching the scene quietly, his expression unreadable, though there's a softness in his eyes that makes me pause. He hasn't said much since the incident earlier, and I wonder if he's still shaken by it.

For a moment, I consider going to him, just to check in, to make sure he's all right, but something stops me. Maybe it's the weariness I feel, or maybe it's the knowledge that tonight isn't the right time for that conversation. I'll speak with him tomorrow.

With a final glance around the room, I slip out, grateful to be free of the ball and its suffocating atmosphere.

It's not just physical exhaustion anymore. It's the frustration of another night spent searching, hoping, and coming up empty-handed. The truth is, I'm tired of waiting. Tired of pretending that everything will work out in its own time. I know I should be patient, that I have years ahead of me, but the sense of urgency I feel is impossible to ignore.

Something is coming, something big, something dangerous, and I need to be ready. But how can I be ready when I haven't even found my One? When my powers remain dormant, waiting for the bond that will awaken them?

I manage to escape to the empty hallway, relieved to finally have a moment of peace. It gives me the space I need to breathe and to think. The night has been overwhelming, to say the least, and it's been completely devoid of the answer I sought.

I don't know when I'll find my One, or if I'll ever find him. But what I do know is that I can't afford to wait forever. Time is running out, and I can feel the pressure building, a storm on the horizon.

For now, though, all I can do is rest. Tomorrow is another day, and maybe, just maybe, it will bring the answers I've been searching for.

I take my leave of the festivities, slipping down the corridor unnoticed. When I finally reach my room, I gratefully collapse in my bed, already wearied from the first ball. It's going to be a long month.

CHAPTER 7

FORMAL APOLOGIES

Maerilee

The next morning, I sit straight-backed in my chair, positioned on the dais next to my mother and father. The throne room feels colder than usual, though that has more to do with the political atmosphere than the physical temperature.

The sun is streaming through the tall windows, casting the room in golden light, but the tension in the room is palpable. My fingers rest on my lap, carefully clasped to avoid betraying any of the unease building in my chest. I'm supposed to be calm, poised. Queenly, as my mother would say.

At my side mother radiates composure. Father sits on her other side, his expression one of polite anticipation, though I know him well enough to see the glint of amusement in his eyes. The situation isn't lost on him, though he'd never show it openly. He wouldn't say it out loud, but he found the entire situation with River and Brook amusing last night. In his mind, it's just a bout of youthful indiscretion.

Of course, that's because he comes from Dearlish, where the

customs are much different. Here, any slight against a future queen is enough to be excommunicated for good.

The heavy doors to the throne room swing open with a creak, and in step King Alastair and Queen Lyria of Oceana, followed by their sons. River walks with his usual swagger, his chin held too high, his nose in the air, while Brook trails behind with his shoulders slightly slumped, as though the weight of his family's embarrassment rests squarely on him. The difference between the two brothers is stark.

They approach, and when they reach the foot of the dais, they bow in unison. I resist the urge to let out a sigh. Formality always feels like an unnecessary prelude to conversations that should be simpler, but I understand its importance. My mother would be proud. This is simply how things are done, and I've long since learned to respect the nuances of diplomacy.

"Your Majesties," King Alastair begins, his voice deep and steady, "we come before you today with sincere regret for the unfortunate events that transpired last night."

Queen Lyria nods beside him, her hands folded neatly in front of her, looking every bit the poised monarch.

"We deeply apologize for the disruption caused by our son, River," she adds, her voice softer but no less firm. "It was never our intention for such an incident to occur at your ball."

I keep my face neutral, though the memory of River's behavior threatens to make me roll my eyes. I glance at Brook, who's standing beside his parents, looking like he's about to crumble under the weight of the apology they're here to offer on his brother's behalf. River is staring ahead, expression blank, though I catch the faintest twitch in his jaw. He's not remotely sorry for what happened, just annoyed that he was caught.

King Alastair turns to his sons.

"Brook, River," he says firmly, the authority in his voice clear. "You owe the princess of Altinna an apology. Now."

Brook immediately steps forward. His gaze is fixed on the floor, and he begins to speak in a voice that's both subdued and apologetic.

"Your Highness, I'm deeply sorry for the disruption last night. It was never my intention for the evening to unfold the way it did. I apologize for any embarrassment caused."

The defeated tone in his voice tugs at something within me, and I can't help but feel a pang of sympathy. Brook didn't do anything wrong. If anything, he saved me from a rather unfortunate situation. I won't let him take the fall for something that wasn't his fault. And I certainly won't let him shoulder River's blame.

"Prince Brook," I interrupt, my voice firm but kind. His head snaps up, surprise flickering in his eyes. "There's no need for you to apologize. In fact, it is I who should be thanking you, again, for saving my dress last night. It was brand new, and if it weren't for your quick thinking, I'd have been drenched in spring wine."

Brook blinks, clearly taken aback. I can see his eyes dart toward his brother before they settle back on me. A faint twinkle appears in them, a spark of something that wasn't there moments ago. Relief, perhaps.

"And, if I may add," I continue, casting a glance toward River, whose expression has darkened considerably. "Redirecting an entire tray of wine with water magic? That's not an easy feat. I imagine it takes much more skill than, say, causing a little bit of frost on the floor."

That does it. River's face turns an angry shade of red, his jaw tightening as he glares at me. He knows exactly what I'm referring to, and he doesn't like being called out in front of everyone. He looks like he's on the verge of saying something, but instead he spins on his heel and storms out of the throne room without a word.

I don't bother hiding my satisfaction. My mother will scold me later, I'm sure, but for now, I feel a small sense of triumph. Brook's eyes are shining now, a faint smile tugging at his lips. I'm glad I could do this small thing for him, even if it means making an enemy of River.

King Alastair and Queen Lyria stand there for a moment, clearly flustered. River's abrupt exit has caught them off guard, and they seem at a loss for how to proceed. Finally, King Alastair clears his throat, his voice stiff and formal once again.

"We deeply apologize for River's behavior," he says, though the words sound hollow. "Rest assured, he will be dealt with."

Queen Lyria nods, her cheeks flushed with embarrassment.

"Yes, we will address this matter immediately," she sputters, her composure nearly gone. "Please accept our sincerest apologies once more, Your Highnesses."

They bow again, though this time their exit is hurried and awkward. Brook trails behind them, his steps slow and measured, as though he's trying to delay the inevitable. As they leave, Brook glances over his shoulder at me, and for a brief moment, our eyes meet. There's a silent gratitude in his gaze, and I can't help but smile in return. He may be forgotten by his parents, overshadowed by his brother, but I won't let him be overlooked here.

Once the Oceanans have left, the throne room feels significantly emptier. The tension that hung in the air has dissipated, replaced by a more relaxed atmosphere. Well, relaxed for some of us.

"Maerilee." My mother's voice is sharp, and I turn to see her giving me a pointed look. "That was unnecessary."

I brace myself for the reprimand. "I was only telling the truth, Mother," I reply, my tone respectful but firm. "Brook didn't deserve to be treated like that, and River—"

"River is not your concern," Kimalissa cuts me off, her eyes narrowing slightly. "It is not your place to get involved in the affairs of another kingdom's princes."

"Not to mention," she adds, her voice softening just slightly, "provoking him in front of his parents was reckless."

I bite the inside of my cheek to keep from arguing further. She's right, of course, but that doesn't mean I regret it. River needed to be put in his place, and Brook needed someone to stand up for him.

Before I can respond, my father chuckles softly from his seat. I glance at him, surprised by the amusement dancing in his eyes.

"Come now, Kimalissa," father says, his voice warm and teasing. "She's got a point. River is a bit of a prat, and someone needed to say it."

My mother shoots him a sharp look, but he merely grins back at her.

"Besides," he adds, still chuckling. "I thought it was rather well played. Very diplomatic, in its own way."

I catch movement out of the corner of my eye and notice Akin standing nearby, his face schooled into a neutral expression. But there's a glimmer in his eyes, too, and the corners of his mouth twitch upward. He's trying very hard not to smile, though he's clearly enjoying the whole thing.

"I suppose," my mother says with a sigh, clearly outnumbered. "But that doesn't change the fact that we must tread carefully with the Oceanans. A misstep could lead to political fallout."

"I'll be more careful next time," I promise, though I know I'll still speak up if I feel it's necessary. My mother knows this, too, and she gives me a look that says as much.

"See that you are," she says, her tone softening slightly. "I know your intentions were good, but we must always think of the bigger picture, Maerilee. The safety of Altinna depends on it."

I nod, understanding her concerns. We're surrounded by kingdoms that would seize any opportunity to weaken us, and the Oceanans are powerful allies. I won't jeopardize that alliance, but that doesn't mean I'll let people like River walk all over others, not even his own brother.

As the room begins to clear, I let out a quiet sigh, feeling the weight of the encounter settle over me. My mother is right in her own way. The world of court politics is delicate, and one wrong move could have lasting consequences. But I also know that we can't ignore what's right in front of us just to maintain appearances. Sometimes, we have to stand up for what's fair, even if it means shaking things up a bit.

CHAPTER 8
WISE COUNSEL

Maerilee

Not an hour later, I watch as the council members file into the chamber, the tension from earlier still lingering in the air. I take my place beside my mother as she stands at the head of the long table. Father is seated next to her, his expression nearly unreadable to others, though I can still see the faint humor in his eyes.

My gaze sweeps over the gathered advisors, familiar faces who have been part of the council for as long as I can remember. Then, a man I don't recognize catches my eye. He's tall, his presence quietly commanding, though he doesn't seem to be trying to draw attention to himself. His hair is dark, falling just past his shoulders, and even from this distance, there's something unsettling about his eyes. Who is he?

Before I can ask, my mother speaks.

"Before we begin," she addresses them, her calm voice commanding the assembly. "We have a new member of the council I'd like to introduce."

I sit up straighter, curiosity piqued. I glance at the unfamiliar man again, and this time, his gaze locks with mine. There's a brief flicker of something that passes between us. It's hard to describe. A pull, a faint sense of recognition, though I'm certain I've never met him before. I feel intrigued, but not in the way my mother has always described I should feel when I find my One. It's different. Subtle. Yet, it's there.

"This is Permiton," my mother continues, gesturing toward the man. "He hails from Ambrosia but has decided to defect to Altinna. He brings with him valuable knowledge and insight."

Defected from Ambrosia? That alone is enough to raise my interest. Prince Direken is from Ambrosia, and their people are notoriously loyal. What could have made him leave?

Mother's next words really catch me off guard.

"He is also a seer," she says, her tone steady, though I catch the faintest hint of caution beneath it.

A seer. My eyes widen slightly as I take that in. Seers are rare, even among the fae, and they hold a power that can change the course of kingdoms. I study Permiton more closely now, my mind racing with questions.

I glance at Eirliwyn, one of our longest-serving advisors, standing on the opposite side of the table. He's always been calm and unflappable, but now, for the first time, I think I see him flinch. It's quick, barely noticeable, but it's there. Why? Eirliwyn has always been one of my mother's most trusted confidantes. He's never been one to react openly, especially not in council.

I brush it off. There are bigger things to focus on.

My gaze shifts back to Permiton, and again, our eyes meet. That strange sensation flares up between us again. It's a spark of curiosity, something I can't explain but can't ignore either. I'm frustrated that the universe keeps teasing me with half-answers. Why can't things just be clear?

Permiton

The moment I step into the throne room, my heart nearly stops. There, seated next to Queen Kimalissa and King Fratino, is the woman who has haunted my dreams for months, though I could never quite see her face clearly until now.

Maerilee.

I'm struck dumb for a moment, barely managing to hold my composure. The sudden realization that she, the princess of Altinna, is the woman my dreams have circled around for so long has me reeling. I can feel the weight of her gaze sweeping across the room, and for a moment, our eyes lock. There's something in our shared look that makes me shiver. It's subtle, almost imperceptible, but it's enough to confirm what I've suspected.

I am not ready for this.

As is always the case with my visions and dreams, I don't understand what it all means yet. They are often jumbled, flashes of future possibilities that only make sense when the events are right in front of me. The universe rarely gives me clear, unambiguous answers. Still, the fact that she's been in my dreams at all must mean something important. Something big. But until I puzzle it out, I can't say a word to her about it.

I take a deep breath, trying to regain my focus. This is not the time to get lost in my own thoughts, not in front of the council. I have a role to play, and I cannot afford to let anyone, even the woman of my dreams, distract me from it.

Queen Kimalissa is speaking, addressing the council about the dangers posed by the visiting dignitaries and nobles, the potential alliances we need to form, and the threats we must be wary of. I listen carefully, my mind racing as I try to keep up with the flow of the conversation. The council is tense, everyone on edge.

I glance at Maerilee again, trying to gauge her reactions. She looks calm, though there's a fire behind her eyes. It's clear she has deep respect for her mother, and a love for her kingdom. I feel an overwhelming urge to protect her. From what, I'm not entirely sure yet.

When the opportunity arises, I clear my throat and speak, my voice steady despite the turmoil inside me.

"Perhaps," I begin, carefully choosing my words, "it would be wise to focus on the well-being of Altinna, rather than entangling ourselves too deeply in the politics of other kingdoms. We must be cautious of those who seek to involve us in their affairs, for they often do so for their own gain, not ours."

The throne room falls silent. Every eye in the room turns toward me, and for a brief moment, I wonder if I've overstepped. Queen Kimalissa's expression is unreadable, though her gaze feels sharper than before. I chance a glance at Maerilee, and she is glaring at me, her eyes narrowing in a way that makes my stomach twist.

I hold my breath, waiting for the queen's response.

After what feels like an eternity, Queen Kimalissa nods slowly.

"Permiton speaks wisely," she says, her voice calm and measured. "Altinna has always been at risk from those who seek to manipulate us for their own ends. We must be vigilant, and we must prioritize our own survival before all else."

The room relaxes somewhat as murmurs of agreement ripple through the council. Yet Maerilee is still glaring at me as though I've insulted her personally. My mind races, trying to figure out what I said that was so wrong.

It takes me a moment to realize it. Of course. I've just told her to stay out of other kingdoms' politics, yet it's her duty to her kingdom to find her One, someone who likely hails from another kingdom.

Damn it.

I want to kick myself for not thinking it through before opening my mouth. I insulted her. And the last thing I wanted to do was alienate the one person in this room I need to understand most.

The meeting continues, but I'm barely paying attention. All I can think about is how to fix this. I watch her, wondering how I can apologize, how I can explain myself without making things worse. But the moment the meeting adjourns, she's on her feet and heading for the door.

"Princess Maerilee, may I have a word?" I call after her, my voice catching in my throat as I hurry to catch up with her. I hate how clumsy my words sound, but I can't let her leave like this.

She turns to look at me, her expression harsh.

"Permiton, was it?" she asks, her voice cool and distant. Gone is the warmth I saw in her eyes earlier, replaced by a wall I'm not sure how to break through.

"Yes," I stutter stupidly. "I-I didn't mean to offend you," I say, my words coming out in a rush. "I just—what I said in there—it wasn't meant as a criticism of you. I was only trying to... I thought—"

She holds up a hand, cutting me off.

"It's fine, Permiton," she answers curtly.

But I can tell it isn't. Her tone is too dismissive, too final. She's brushing me off, and I don't blame her. I probably sound like an idiot, stumbling over my words like this. Why is it so hard to talk to her?

"Please, just listen," I say, more desperate now. "I didn't mean to suggest that what you're doing isn't important. I know you're doing everything you can for Altinna. I just... I've seen things. In my visions. Things that make me think we need to be careful, that's all. I didn't mean to undermine you."

For a moment, I think I see something soften in her eyes, but it's gone just as quickly.

"I appreciate your concern, Permiton," she says, her voice still cool but less harsh now. "You do your duties for the kingdom, and I'll do mine."

With that, she turns and walks away, leaving me standing there, feeling like a complete fool.

I watch her go, frustration and regret churning in my gut. I meant well. I always mean well. But somehow, I've managed to make things worse between us. And now, I'm left with more questions than answers.

Who is Maerilee, really? And why can't I shake the feeling that my dreams about her are only just beginning?

CHAPTER 9
BARRIERS

Maerilee

My pulse races as I storm out of the council meeting, the heavy doors slamming behind me. I don't bother slowing down, my steps quick and sharp as I head toward the gardens. Stifling air presses in on me, the weight of Permiton's words echoing in my mind. Who does he think he is anyway? Even if he is a seer, he's new to the council. He had no right to interject his thoughts so soon.

The moment I reach the gardens, the cool air and scent of blossoms offer a brief, fragile reprieve. My spot among the flowers, where I've sought solace more times than I can count, is just ahead. I quicken my pace, eager to be enveloped in the calming silence of nature, away from politics, away from expectations, away from everything.

But when I round the final bend, I freeze.

There, lounging in the middle of my sanctuary, is River of all people. Of course he is. Because my morning isn't annoying enough. He's leaning casually near the coneflowers, looking every bit the arrogant fool I know him to be, his dark hair tousled just enough to appear careless, though I'm sure he spent ages perfecting that effortless charm.

For a heartbeat, I think about turning around, finding a different path, somewhere else to decompress. But as soon as I pivot on my heel, his voice reaches me.

"Is that Princess Maerilee I spot? Leaving so soon?" His tone drips with a smarmy arrogance that I can't stand.

My jaw clenches, and I spin back toward him, my eyes narrowing.

"This is my sanctuary, River. What are you doing here?"

"Surely, you wouldn't deny the beautiful amenities of your garden to your honored guests," he smirks, straightening and sauntering toward me. "That wouldn't be very diplomatic of you, would it, Maerilee?"

There's something about the way he says my name, a sly mockery in every syllable, that makes my blood boil.

I glare at him, refusing to rise to his bait.

"These are my private gardens," I seethe. "I don't need to explain myself to you."

"Your private gardens?" He looks around with an exaggerated gesture. "You really should hang a sign somewhere. Any old riff-raff could wander in."

My hands clench into fists. The urge to shout at him, to scream, is overwhelming, but I can't give him that satisfaction.

"Please leave, River."

Instead of cooperating, he steps closer, blocking my path. His smirk deepens.

"Touchy today, aren't we? You had a council meeting today, if I remember correctly. Let me guess—the mighty council is doubting their future queen again?"

He's too close now, far too close. The scent of salt and sea air that clings to him mixes with the floral scent of the garden. It's suffocating. I take a step back, trying to create space, but the heat between us doesn't dissipate. I don't know if it's anger or something else, something I refuse to acknowledge.

"You wouldn't understand," I snap, folding my arms defensively. "You don't take anything seriously, least of all your own duties."

River raises an eyebrow and clutches his hand to his chest in mock offense.

"That hurts, Princess. Truly. You wound me."

"I'm sure you'll recover," I bite out, my patience hanging by a thread. "Just go back to your meaningless flirtations and leave me in peace."

His grin falters slightly, and something flickers in his eyes, but it's gone too fast for me to read.

"Meaningless, huh? Maybe I'm just waiting for someone worthy of my attention."

I snort, unable to help myself.

"Is that what you call it? Chasing after every woman you lay eyes on is your version of waiting?"

He moves closer again, until there's only a breath of space between us. His voice drops, low and teasing.

"Jealous, are we?"

Heat floods my cheeks, and I can't tell if it's from rage or embarrassment. I step forward, closing the gap, my face just inches from his.

"Jealous? Of you? Don't make me laugh."

There's a moment where we're staring at each other, neither backing down. His eyes, dark as the depths of the ocean, meet mine, and something shifts in the air between us. My heart is pounding now, but not with anger.

And then, before I can think or react, he closes the gap between us and kisses me.

The world tilts. It's as if the ground disappears beneath me, and all that's left is the feel of his lips on mine, surprisingly soft, surprisingly warm. His hands grip my arms, and for a moment, I kiss him back. There's a fire there, one I didn't expect, one that consumes everything else.

Then reality crashes in.

What am I doing?

With a sharp gasp, I pull away, shoving him back as if he's burned me. My breath comes in shallow, panicked bursts, my heart racing for entirely different reasons now. River stands there, stunned, his lips parted in disbelief.

"What?" he stammers, his usual arrogance completely shattered.

But I can't process his reaction because that's when I feel the barrier. Between us, I've erected a shimmering, impenetrable wall of energy. I can feel it as if it's another limb. My magic.

Oh no.

I step back, shaking my head, trying to push the realization away, but the truth is undeniable. This shouldn't have happened. This couldn't have happened. But it did. I erected a barrier between us. That only happens with someone who—

No. No, no, no. He can't be.

River's eyes widen as he senses the magic, his hand pressing against the invisible wall. "Maerilee... what is this?"

I back away, heart hammering in my chest. "It's nothing," I choke out, my voice trembling. "This... this isn't possible."

"I don't know what this is, but it's not what you think," I lie, my voice cracking. "Stay away from me."

Without waiting for his response, I turn and run, the pounding of my footsteps drowned out by the pounding in my chest. I can't look back. I can't face what this means.

Not him. Not River.

Please, not him.

River

My heart is pounding. I've kissed plenty of women before, but this felt different. I've never experienced anything like it. The ground itself shifted under me for a second. My lips are still tingling, my skin buzzing, and it's not just the kiss. There's something else. Power.

I frown, looking down at my hands. They're shaking, and there's a strange pull in my chest, like something just woke up inside me. Something vast and unfamiliar. My magic has always been tied to water. Oceana runs in my veins, after all. This is different. This feels deeper, stronger.

My gaze drifts over to the coneflowers, still standing tall in the garden, unaware of the chaos running through me. I take a step closer, extending a hand, curious. The energy swirling inside me shifts, like it's begging to be used. I've always been able to summon water from a nearby source, but this feels different. I can feel moisture in the air itself, waiting, ready to obey.

I extend my hand over the flowers, focusing on the pull inside me. A second passes, and then another, before the sky above responds. Rain falls, not in delicate drops, but in a sudden downpour, drenching the flowers and the ground beneath my feet. I watch in stunned silence as the rain cascades down, soaking everything in its path.

I've never conjured rain like this before. Not out of nowhere. Not without effort. I curl my fingers, drawing the rain back, and as easily as it began, it stops. The storm clouds vanish, and the garden is still again, save for the dripping leaves and puddles forming in the dirt.

A grin spreads across my face. Power like that? I could get used to it. No need to rely on the ocean or a nearby stream when I can summon a storm with a flick of my wrist. I feel invincible.

Then the realization slams into me like a wave, and the grin slips right off my face.

No.

I stumble back, my heart racing for an entirely different reason now. This kind of power can only mean one thing. I rub my face with both hands, trying to scrub away the thought, but it's lodged there now.

I'm her One.

I close my eyes, groaning. Of all the women in Haebradia, it has to be her? I let out a humorless laugh, pacing back and forth in the garden.

It couldn't be anyone simple, could it? Couldn't be one of the dozens of women I've flirted with over the years. No, it has to be the one woman who probably hates me more than anyone.

The idea of being tied to Maerilee—permanently—is unsettling, to say the least. Sure, she's beautiful. That's undeniable. But she's also infuriating. Stubborn. Always ready to challenge me at every turn. And now, if I'm really her One, we're bound by something bigger than either of us. Something I can't flirt my way out of.

I take a deep breath, staring up at the sky as the last of the clouds drift away.

What the hell am I supposed to do now?

CHAPTER 10
MOUNTING FRUSTRATION

Maerilee

I throw myself onto my bed, face-first into the pillows, and scream as loudly as I can. My voice muffles into the fabric, but it doesn't stop the frustration, the disbelief, the absolute rage building in me. My legs kick out violently, my fists pound into the bed, and I keep screaming until my throat feels raw and my chest is burning.

River. River. How could this be happening? Of all the people in the world, of all the fae, it's him? The arrogant, smug River? No. It's impossible.

He can't be my One, he just can't.

I flip over, grabbing another pillow and pressing it to my face, screaming again. Hot tears burn at the corners of my eyes, but I refuse to let them fall. I won't cry over this. I can't. But the anger swirling in my chest feels too big, too overwhelming.

How could this happen to me?

I roll over onto my back, staring up at the ceiling as if I might find answers in the intricate patterns carved there. I don't know what to think, what to feel.

I shove the pillow off the bed and let out a long, frustrated groan. Why River of all people? His smug face, the way he always seems to know how to get under my skin, like it's a game to him. Maybe even this is a game to him.

I try to push the memory of our kiss out of my mind, but it's impossible. The way his lips felt against mine, the way my whole body reacted.

"No," I whisper to myself, my voice hoarse. "It wasn't real. It can't be real."

A knock sounds at the door, soft but insistent.

"Maerilee?" Akin's voice. Gentle, concerned, steady.

I squeeze my eyes shut, trying to block it out. I don't want to see anyone right now, least of all Akin.

He knocks again, a little louder this time. "Maerilee, please. I'm coming in."

I hear the door creak open, but I don't move. I stay on my back, staring at the ceiling, refusing to look at him.

"Are you okay?" Akin's voice is closer now, full of concern. I feel the bed dip slightly as he sits on the edge, but I still don't look at him.

"No," I say, my voice sharp. "I'm not okay."

There's silence for a moment, and I can feel him watching me. Waiting.

"Do you want to talk about it?" he asks quietly.

I let out a bitter laugh.

"What's there to talk about?" I sit up suddenly, turning to face him. "You already know what happened, don't you? Everyone probably knows by now."

Akin shakes his head.

"I don't know what you're talking about, Maerilee. I swear."

I narrow my eyes at him.

"Oh, really? So the fact that I kissed River, the fact that I felt something, no one's talking about that?"

He blinks, clearly taken aback.

"You kissed him?" His tone is a mixture of disgust and hurt.

I scoff, folding my arms across my chest.

"It wasn't on purpose. It just kind of happened. And now..." I trail off, feeling the anger rise in my throat again. "Now I don't know what's going on. But he can't be my One, Akin. He just can't."

Akin looks at me, his expression unreadable.

"Why not?" he asks, more gently.

"Why not?" I repeat, my voice rising. "Because he's River! Because he's arrogant, and infuriating, and..." I stumble over my words, not sure how to explain the rest.

Akin is quiet for a long moment. Then he says, "Maybe it's a good thing, Maerilee. Maybe finding your One—whoever he is—will help you. Help the kingdom."

I stare at him, feeling my chest tighten. He's right, of course. Finding my One would strengthen me, unlock powers I don't fully understand. Yet, there's something in his expression that I can't miss.

I've seen it before, of course. I've always been aware of the way he looks at me when he thinks I'm not paying attention. The secret is, I'm always paying attention to him, always hoping foolishly. Even without the pull I'm supposed to feel toward him, I've always secretly hoped that Akin could be it for me.

"Do you really think that?" I ask, my voice quieter now, more fragile. "Do you really think this is a good thing?"

Akin opens his mouth to answer, but the words seem to catch in his throat. I see it in his eyes, the struggle, the hesitation. He's trying to say what he thinks is best for me, for the kingdom. But I know him too well.

"Akin," I say softly, my heart pounding in my chest. "Do you really mean that?"

He looks away, jaw clenched, his hands fisting in his lap. There's a long, tense silence before he finally speaks.

"No," he whispers, barely audible. Then, louder, "No, I don't."

Before I can respond, he stands abruptly and moves closer to me. His eyes are dark, filled with something I've never seen before.

He grabs my face in his hands, pulling me toward him, and before I can say anything, his lips crash against mine. It's fierce, desperate, and I'm so shocked that for a moment, I don't react. But then I feel it, a spark, a tingle running through me, something powerful and electric.

My hands move on their own, clutching at his arms as he kisses me, and for a moment, the world seems to fall away. There's nothing but him, the heat of his mouth on mine, the way his hands tighten on my skin.

But then I pull back, gasping for air, staring up at him in confusion.

"Akin," I whisper, my voice trembling, unable to say anything else.

He looks down at me, breathing hard, his eyes filled with something I can't quite place. Fear? Regret?

"I shouldn't have done that," he says, his voice hoarse. "I shouldn't have…"

He turns away from me, heading toward the door.

"Wait," I call after him, my heart racing. "Don't go."

He stops, his back to me, one hand resting on the doorframe. I can see the tension in his shoulders, the way he's fighting with himself.

"Akin, please," I say, my voice softer now, almost pleading. "I don't want you to leave."

For a moment, he doesn't move. Then, slowly, he reaches toward the door and turns the lock. He faces me, his eyes locking with mine. There's a storm of emotions swirling in them—desire, guilt, something else I can't quite name.

He walks back to the bed, his steps slow, deliberate. When he reaches me, he doesn't say a word. He just looks at me, waiting.

I swallow hard, feeling my pulse quicken. "Stay," I whisper, my voice barely audible.

He simply nods and sits on the bed, his hands moving to my hips so he can lift me over him. I straddle his waist, the evidence of his desire already growing, and I press my body against his, shivering at the contact. I've never been with a man like this, never felt this kind of heat from the top of my head to the soles of my feet.

Akin groans as his lips meet mine, tenderly at first. We're a jumble of limbs and lips and sweet words that escape us before we have a chance to take them back. He lifts the hem of my dress, his hands scraping the sides of my thighs as he goes, and I feel an unearthly heat growing at my core.

This is nothing like my mother described, but I can't imagine her ever telling me about something as private as this. He pulls my dress over my head so that I'm nearly bare in front of him. His hands nimbly move to my back as I feel him struggling with the strings of my corset.

I kiss his mouth, his cheek, his neck, anything I can reach as I wait impatiently to be revealed to him. Then it occurs to me that there are parts of him I would also very much like to see. I fiddle with the buttons of his shirt, opening it up to reveal a strong chest. I kiss every inch of skin, growing more desperate for him as he moans my name.

Finally, my corset loosens, pinned between our bodies. I reluctantly pull away so he can discard it, needing to feel his skin on mine. Before I'm blessed with that feeling though, he flips us so that I'm lying on my back with him hovering above. In this position, I'm vulnerable to him in a way I've never been, yet I trust him completely. Whatever he wants, whatever he asks of me, I will give it without question.

He groans louder as his eyes rake over my naked form, and I've never felt so alive, so beautiful, so impatient. I don't want to wait any longer for whatever is going to happen between us. I pull his face to mine, kissing him deeply, eagerly. His fingers trace my inner thigh, then move to my entrance, so hesitant, but so wanting.

"You must stop me," he gasps reluctantly. "Tell me this isn't what you want, Maerilee, I'll walk away from you forever, I swear it."

I kiss him deeply, my tongue colliding with his, giving him whatever answer he needs. And then I feel him moving between my legs, before he fills me, sheathing himself inside of me. I scream out from the bizarre pleasure of it, needing so much more of him than I can possibly express in words. And he gives himself fully.

CHAPTER 11

COMPLICATIONS

Maerilee

I wake up slowly, feeling a warmth that isn't just from the morning sun filtering through the curtains. There's a weight pressed against me, solid and comforting, and as I blink the sleep from my eyes, I realize Akin's arm is draped across my waist, his naked body flush against mine. For a moment, I lie still, letting the contentment wash over me as I recall the events of last night. It's a feeling I haven't experienced before, this sense of peace, of belonging to someone completely. My heart flutters, and I wonder if maybe, just maybe, I've found what I've been searching for all along.

Could it really be this simple? Could Akin be my One?

It doesn't make sense that it's taken so long for us to find each other, though. I've seen Akin nearly every single day of my life. Why have I never felt that feeling of absolute certainty that my mother always described? Why have my powers not manifested until now? I try to not think about it too much as I feel his body move against mine and just try to enjoy the pleasure of it.

Then River's face pops into my mind, and I'm reminded of the slight surge of power I felt when I was around him. The thought sends a ripple of uncertainty through me. I remember the ball the other night, the endless circling through the crowd without a single blip of any feeling. Then the momentary flicker of something when I looked at River. I'd thought I felt a spark then, the panic at that spark, making me wonder if he was the One I'd been waiting for.

At the time, the mere thought of River being my One was horrifying. He was and still is the last person I could ever want to be with. Akin makes sense for me. There's always been an attraction there, even if we both pushed it away.

Then why did your powers never manifest? Why did you feel something when you looked into River's eyes?

I try to vanquish the thoughts. Lying here in Akin's arms, he's all I want to think about, all I want to focus on.

Maybe I'd just imagined a spark with River. Maybe my powers strengthened simply because Akin was close by, offering me his steady, unwavering presence.

I flex my fingers, feeling the energy hum beneath my skin, and I can't help but test it out. My eyes land on Duchess's ball lying on the floor. With a small smile, I focus on it, letting my magic unfurl gently from my fingertips. A barrier forms around the ball, shimmering faintly in the morning light. I imagine it moving, and with a tiny push of will, the ball begins to roll across the floor.

Duchess, who had been snoozing contentedly at the foot of the bed, suddenly perks up. Her ears twitch, and within seconds, she's off the bed, chasing after the ball with her usual enthusiasm. But this time, when she reaches it, her teeth snap at empty air, the barrier keeping the ball just out of her reach. She circles it, paws at it, even tries nudging it with her nose, but the barrier holds firm.

I giggle softly, watching as she tries again and again to get her little mouth around the ball, her frustration growing with each failed attempt. Pride and relief swell within me in equal measures. Akin has done this. He's the reason I'm able to access my powers now. I'll finally be able to protect the kingdom, to help Mother secure the boundary. All is finally right in my world.

The man himself stirs beside me, and I glance over to find him watching me with a lazy smile, his eyes warm and filled with a tenderness that makes my heart skip a beat. He doesn't say anything at first, just takes in the scene of me, Duchess, and the ball moving in circles under my control. I'm reminded of when he walked in on me the other day, witnessing my utter failure.

What's changed between then and now? A traitorous voice in my head asks. I try to hide my inner turmoil from him, wanting only to bask in the serenity of being in his presence.

"Good morning," he whispers, pressing his lips gently against my bare shoulder.

"Hi," I whisper back, feeling almost shy, despite the intimacy we shared the previous evening. "Last night was amazing."

I feel him smile against me and we sit there for a moment, just wrapped around each other.

"Do you think I'm your One?" he asks after a while, his voice low and gentle, yet tinged with something I can't quite place.

I turn to look at him, holding his gaze, my heart racing as I consider his question. Everything about this moment feels right, like it's exactly where I'm supposed to be. Yet I'm still plagued with so many questions, so many doubts. Everything simultaneously feels exactly right and completely out of control. When I stare into his eyes, though, I see everything I can ever want. And that has to be enough.

"I do," I say softly, pushing aside any lingering doubts. "I really do."

He sighs, the sound heavy with a mix of relief and something else.

"What are we going to tell your parents?" he asks, his brow furrowing slightly. "I'm a bodyguard, Maerilee. Not a noble. They might not—"

"They'll be happy I've found my One," I interrupt, reaching up to touch his cheek, feeling the stubble beneath my fingers. "That's all that matters to them. That's all that matters to me."

His insecurity is evident in his expression, but I want to wipe it away. In this bed, wrapped around him so tenderly, I want to show him exactly how desperate I am for him to be my One. Akin closes his eyes, leaning into my touch, and for a moment, everything feels perfect. I'm about to say more, to reassure him that this is exactly what we both deserve, when a loud, insistent banging on my door shatters the quiet.

We both jerk upright, and I feel Akin's muscles tense as the knocking continues.

"Maerilee!" River's voice calls from the other side of the door, loud and demanding. "We need to talk."

I groan inwardly, exchanging a glance with Akin. His expression is a mix of concern and annoyance, mirroring my own feelings perfectly. I don't want to deal with River right now, not when I've just discovered something so precious. But I know he's not going to go away easily.

"Go away, River," I shout back, keeping my voice steady despite the irritation bubbling beneath the surface.

River will not be so easily turned away, I know that. He's far too annoying to do anything I ask him to do. I don't want to face him, though. Not now. Not with so many questions circling in my head. All I want right now is to crawl back under the covers with Akin and explore more of our connection.

But, of course, River isn't inclined to give me what I want.

"Maerilee, it's important," he bellows again through the door. "I hate this as much as you do, but I think I'm your One."

Akin and I lock eyes for a moment, before we burst into quiet laughter. Thank goodness I have him beside me to help dispel any fears that River could be right.

"I'm afraid I've already found my One," I shout back, staring deeply into Akin's eyes. "So you and I have absolutely nothing to discuss."

There's a brief pause, and for a moment, I think he might actually leave. But then, without warning, the sound of rain begins to patter against the floor, not from outside, but from directly above us. My heart leaps into my throat as droplets of water start to fall from the ceiling, soaking the bed and sending Duchess yelping under the bed in a panic.

"What the—" I gasp, scrambling to my feet as the rain turns into a downpour, drenching everything in the room. Akin jumps up beside me, his face darkening with anger.

"River!" I shout, wiping the water from my eyes as I glare at the door. "Stop this right now!"

But the rain continues, relentless and cold, soaking through my clothes and turning the once-cozy room into a chaotic mess. I can hear Duchess whining from under the bed, clearly terrified by the sudden onslaught of water.

"Like I said," River shouts through the door, loud enough to be heard over the torrential downpour. "You and I need to talk."

Akin and I exchange a look, and he nods, giving me silent permission to speak with River.

"Fine," I scream. "Just stop the damn rain!"

The water immediately stops, leaving everything drenched in its path.

CHAPTER 12

NOTHING MAKES SENSE

Maerilee

I yank open the wardrobe, my hands trembling slightly as I sift through the dry clothes. I'm going to kill River for this. Duchess is still hiding under the bed. I grab a simple dress and some undergarments, my fingers brushing against the soft fabric as I pull them out, my heart racing with anxiety about what this could mean.

Akin is standing beside me, quietly changing out of his soaked clothes. I glance at him, my chest tightening with a mixture of emotions I can't quite name. I know what I felt with him, the certainty that settled in my bones when I woke up wrapped in his arms. But there's obviously something deeper going on with River. My destroyed room is proof of that.

Once I'm dressed, I march to the door, pulling it open just enough to slip through and quickly close it behind me. I hear Akin moving inside, the rustle of fabric as he finishes dressing. I hope he stays put. I need a moment to confront River alone, without making this situation even more complicated.

Of course, the moment I step into the hallway, River is there, leaning casually against the wall, his arms crossed over his chest. His eyes flicker with a mix of amusement and irritation, and I can tell I didn't quite close the door quickly enough.

"What's going on, Maerilee?" he demands, his voice low but edged with something dangerous. "Why is your bodyguard half-naked in your room?"

I meet his gaze head-on, refusing to back down.

"I've discovered Akin is my One," I say, the words coming out stronger than I feel. "So, as I already told you, we have nothing else to discuss."

River blinks, and then he laughs, the sound rich and disbelieving.

"Impossible," he scoffs, shaking his head. "As always, you're mistaken, Maerilee. I'm your One. Not some—" he gestures vaguely toward the door, "—servant."

I bristle at his dismissal of Akin, my temper flaring again. "You don't know that. You can't just decide you're my One because it's convenient for you."

He pushes off the wall, stepping closer, and I can see the determination in his eyes.

"It's not about convenience," he growls. "I felt it last night, and I know you did too. You can't just ignore that."

I open my mouth to argue, but before I can say anything, River reaches out and pulls me toward him, his lips crashing down on mine. I freeze, caught off guard by the suddenness of it, and then I feel it. A surge of power, strong and undeniable, floods through me. It's like a jolt to my very core, making my magic hum with intensity. I gasp against his lips, my hands instinctively gripping his arms as I try to steady myself.

When he pulls back, his eyes are alight with something fierce and certain.

"See? You felt that, didn't you?" he asks, his voice breathless. "There's no denying it, Maerilee. I'm your One."

I stumble back, my mind reeling. I did feel it. The power was there, even stronger than it was with Akin. But how can that be? I don't want it to be true. I don't want River to be my One. Akin has to be it, right?

Yet there's no denying the strength of what I just felt.

River watches me, his expression triumphant, as if he's already won.

"I feel it too," he says, his tone softer now, more persuasive. "When I'm with you, my power increases. You wouldn't believe what I'm capable of because of you. Imagine what will happen when we're actually together."

I shake my head, trying to make sense of it all.

"My magic got stronger with Akin," I shoot back defensively. "You can't both be my One. I don't understand what's going on, River, but you're obviously mistaken."

River's smile falters, replaced by a look of confusion.

"What do you mean your magic got stronger with him? That can't be right."

He starts pacing, his face darkened by his confusion. He's trying to puzzle it all out, to find a solution when there's none to be found. Frankly, it's frustrating me that he's treating me as if I'm his problem to solve. It's like he's already decided that I belong to him, when I've made no such indication. I'd rather die.

Akin

I step out of the room, closing the door gently behind me, and find River pacing, his face brooding. His posture is tense, his fists clenched at his sides, and I immediately feel protective of Maerilee. Anger radiates off him in waves, but I refuse to let it intimidate me. I've dealt with men like River my entire life. He's entitled, arrogant, and used to getting his own way. But he won't get his way when it comes to her. She's mine.

I walk up to him, keeping my voice calm, but firm.

"River, I think it's time you left. Maerilee clearly doesn't want to talk to you right now."

His eyes narrow, and he takes a step closer, refusing to back down.

"You don't get to tell me what to do, servant," he snaps. "I'm her One. Not you."

I meet his gaze steadily, my voice still polite, but with a hard edge.

"Whether or not you're her One is something we'll figure out. But right now, you're upsetting her. So, I'm asking you to leave."

River's jaw tightens, and I can see the fury in his eyes, the frustration at not being able to control the situation. He's used to people bending to his will, and the fact that I'm standing in his way is clearly infuriating him.

"I'm not going anywhere," he says through gritted teeth. "Maerilee and I clearly have a lot to figure out, and I'm not letting her damn bodyguard stop me."

He spits at me, causing me to jump back. Entitled prick. I feel my own temper rising, the protective instinct flaring up inside me. I don't care what he says to me, but if this is how he treats those he considers beneath him, there's no telling how he would treat Maerilee if he were given the chance to be alone with her.

He's not going to get that chance. No matter what he may believe in his delusional, arrogant head, I am her One. She's more powerful when she's with me, and I know that must eat him alive. It gives me no small amount of satisfaction to know that he's lost out to someone he considers to be the help.

"You're not listening," I say, my voice lowering so that he has to lean in to hear me. "I'm not asking you. I'm telling you. Leave. Now."

River steps forward, getting in my face, and for a moment, it feels like we're on the brink of a fight. My muscles tense, ready for whatever comes next. I won't let him bully his way through this. Not when Maerilee's well-being is at stake.

"Do you really think you can take me, Akin?" River growls, his eyes burning with challenge. "You're just a bodyguard. I'm a Crown Prince. I have power you can't even begin to understand."

I laugh out loud, as if I'm going to be intimidated by this prissy man-child.

"In hand-to-hand combat, you'd lose every time," I warn. "I've been trained to take down the most cunning assassins. You think a little bitch boy from a nowhere kingdom is going to intimidate me? You're sorely mistaken."

River clenches his fist, clearly ready to swing. I ready myself for the fight, my body tense, my stance defensive. I can take him out in one move if I need to. He doesn't stand a chance against me, and we both know it.

Before the tension can snap, before either of us can make a move, Maerilee's voice cuts through the air, sharp and commanding.

"Stop it, both of you!" she screeches.

We both turn to see her still standing in the doorway, her expression fierce and determined. She steps between us, putting herself directly in the line of fire, and looks at each of us in turn.

"This isn't helping," she says firmly. "We're not going to solve anything by fighting. We need to figure out what's going on, and the only way to do that is to talk to my mother. She'll know what to do."

River bristles, but he doesn't argue. He knows Maerilee is right, and as much as it galls him, he has no choice but to listen.

I nod, taking a step back, though I keep my eyes on River, making sure he knows I'm not backing down, just deferring to Maerilee's wisdom.

"Fine," River mutters, his voice tight with frustration. "Let's go see the queen."

And with that, the three of us head toward the throne room, the tension still thick between us, but at least for now, the fight is on hold.

CHAPTER 13

MOTHER KNOWS BEST?

Maerilee

We walk through the palace corridors in tense silence, River on one side of me and Akin on the other. The air between them is charged, both men radiating barely concealed frustration. I keep my head high, trying to focus on the task at hand. My mother will surely have the answer to this. She'll know what to do.

The weight of the situation presses down on my chest, and I can still feel the remnants of River's kiss, the surge of power I don't fully understand. But there's no time to dwell on that. Not now.

When we finally reach the throne room, I pause just outside the grand doors, the echo of raised voices reaching my ears. My mother's voice, tight with anger, is unmistakable. I motion for Akin and River to stop, pressing my hand lightly against the door to listen. I can hear another voice too, one that sends a chill down my spine.

Direken.

He's here, talking to my mother. No, not just talking, arguing. Heatedly.

"We've waited long enough, Queen Kimalissa," Direken snaps. His voice is sharp, venomous, and filled with barely-concealed malice. "You can't keep stalling. Everyone knows the barrier is weakening, and once it fails, Altinna will fall. Your kingdom is vulnerable."

My breath catches in my throat, and I glance at Akin and River, both of whom are frowning, clearly having heard the same thing. Direken isn't just here for a diplomatic visit. He's threatening my mother.

"I've heard enough of your thinly-veiled threats, Direken," Kimalissa responds, her voice steely and calm, though I can hear the tension in it. "Altinna will stand, as it always has. You'll do well to remember that."

Direken's laugh is dark, mocking. "For how long, Kimalissa? You're running out of time, and everyone knows it. When the barrier crumbles, my armies will be at your doorstep. You can try to hold them off, but we both know you won't succeed."

I grip the doorframe tightly, my heart racing. My mother has always been able to hold her own, but this is different. This is a direct threat against our kingdom. Against *her*. I want to burst through the door and confront Direken myself, but I can't. Not without giving away that we've overheard everything.

Mother's voice cuts through the air like the crack of a whip.

"You will leave now, Direken, and you will not return unless you are prepared to act in good faith."

There's a long pause, and I can almost feel the fury radiating from Direken on the other side of the door. Then, finally, he speaks again, his voice low and dangerous.

"You'll regret this, Kimalissa. You and I both know you're weak."

I hear the sound of footsteps, heavy and deliberate, heading toward the door. My heart leaps into my throat, and I step back quickly, motioning for Akin and River to do the same. We move to the side just as the door swings open and Direken strides out, his face twisted into a mask of anger. He doesn't notice us at first, his gaze fixed ahead, but as he storms past, he catches sight of me. His eyes narrow, and for a moment, I think he might say something, but he just sneers and continues on his way, disappearing down the corridor.

I exhale slowly, trying to calm the rapid beating of my heart. Akin and River exchange a look, and I give them a subtle nod, silently warning them not to say anything about what we just overheard. Mother would not take kindly to us eavesdropping.

With a deep breath, I push open the door to the throne room and step inside, Akin and River following closely behind. My mother is standing by the window, her back to us, the tension still evident in the tight set of her shoulders. The air in the room is thick with the remnants of the heated exchange and I can tell she's still furious.

"Mother," I say gently, stepping forward.

She turns, her expression softening when she sees me. But there's still a shadow in her eyes, a heaviness that wasn't there before.

"Maerilee," she says, her voice warmer than it had been moments ago. "What brings you here?"

She seems to just notice then that I'm not alone, and she looks between Akin, River, and me with increased curiosity.

I exchange a glance with Akin and River, then turn back to my mother.

"Something's happened," I start hesitantly, not even sure how to put this into words. There are some things that feel too delicate to discuss with your mother. But I power through it. "The three of us need to speak with you about it."

Mother's eyes flick to Akin and River, and I can see the questions forming in her mind. She gestures for us to come closer, moving to sit on the edge of her throne.

"Out with it, then," she demands impatiently. "Tell me what's going on."

I take a deep breath, steadying myself before I begin.

"It's about my One. Or rather . . . my Ones." I glance at Akin and then at River, my heart racing as I try to explain the situation as clearly as possible. "I thought Akin was my One. I felt the connection, the power, everything. But then something happened with River."

Mother frowns, confusion flashing across her face.

"What do you mean, something happened with River?"

She shoots him a suspicious look, and I feel a bit vindicated in my dislike for him. He certainly hasn't made a good impression on any of us in his short time here. I can tell from my mother's expression that she doesn't want him as my One any more than I do.

"When he kissed me," I press on, ignoring the way Akin tenses slightly beside me, "I felt the same surge of power I felt with Akin. It was the same, perhaps slightly stronger. I don't understand it, Mother. How can I feel that with both of them? It's supposed to be just one, isn't it?"

For a moment, my mother is silent, her brow furrowed in thought. I can see the wheels turning in her mind as she tries to make sense of what I've just told her. Finally, she shakes her head slightly, her voice soft with uncertainty.

"I don't know, Maerilee," she answers. "This isn't something I've encountered before. The bond is supposed to be singular, a connection between one fae and their One. But if you're feeling it with both Akin and River..." She trails off, looking more troubled than I've ever seen her.

I swallow hard, the weight of the situation pressing down on me. "What do we do?"

Her eyes meet mine, and I can see the worry there, the uncertainty.

"This is beyond anything I can answer alone," she says quietly. "We'll need to bring this before the Council. Perhaps one of the advisors will know more about this, or there may be records of something like this happening before."

I nod, though the thought of involving the Council makes me nervous. They're a group of powerful, wise fae, but they're also deeply rooted in tradition. What will they think of me having two potential Ones? Will they see it as a blessing, or something dangerous?

"I'll call the Council together immediately," Mother continues, sinking down onto her throne and rubbing her temples. "This matter needs to be addressed as soon as possible."

I glance at Akin and River, both who are standing quietly beside me, shockingly patient in Mother's presence. Akin's face is calm, but I can see the tension in his jaw, the worry in his eyes. River, on the other hand, looks more frustrated than anything else, his arms crossed over his chest, his expression stormy. This situation isn't easy on any of us, and it's even more strained without clear answers.

A thought occurs that causes a sinking pit in my stomach. The Council may not be of any more help than Mother is. I've somehow always known I was slightly different than everyone else. My powers have always been especially weak on their own, in more need of nurturing than anyone else's. I've waited all this time to find my One without much hope that he would actually appear.

Now that there are two potentials in the running, I'm even more sure that there's something wrong with me. And if the Council realizes that as well, they may see me as a threat to the future of Altinna. I'm meant to be queen one day, to take charge of the security of this nation and lead it to prosperity. If I can't even handle the simple task of securing my One, how will they ever trust me to lead them?

My anxiety only grows as Mother sends word for an emergency meeting, and I feel the calming presence of Akin to one side, and the irritating presence of River to the other. If I'm forced to choose between either of them, it's no question who I'll pick. I detest River with every fiber of my being. What scares me the most is that the Council will likely see him as the better fit for the kingdom.

I'm terrified of what comes next.

CHAPTER 14

NOT SO UNPRECEDENTED

Maerilee

The throne room is heavy with anticipation as we all sit before the council, the weight of the situation pressing down on me like a ton of bricks. My mother is seated beside me, her expression calm and composed, though I know her well enough to see the worry etched in the tightness around her eyes. My father has joined us, sitting on her other side and completely clueless as to why the meeting has been called. Across from us, River and his parents are seated with an air of restrained authority. Brook, as usual, trails silently along with them, his presence almost forgotten in the midst of everything. Next to me sits Akin, a steady presence in the whirlwind of uncertainty that surrounds us.

The council members are gathered around the long table in the center of the room, their robes of office billowing slightly as they shift in their seats. There's a murmur of conversation as they glance between one another, clearly unsure of how to proceed with the situation we've presented them.

My mother speaks first, her authoritative voice somehow managing to remain gentle.

"I have asked you here today to help us navigate this unprecedented situation," she starts calmly, though I don't miss the flash of concern in her expression. "Princess Maerilee has discovered that she has not one, but two potential Ones. This is unique, to say the least, and we are in need of your guidance."

The room falls silent, the council members exchanging looks of varying degrees of confusion and concern. Finally, one of them, a fae with a stern face and sharp eyes, clears his throat and speaks

"This is indeed a most unusual situation," he begins, his voice clipped and formal. "The bond between a fae and their One is meant to be singular, a unique connection that strengthens both individuals. To have two such bonds . . .," he trails off. "Well, it raises many questions about the validity of either."

Another council member, a woman with silver hair braided intricately around her head, leans forward.

"If Maerilee were to ascend the throne with more than one One, it could create a political and magical imbalance," her voice is commanding and firm. "The laws of succession are clear: the fae who ascends must be bonded to a single One to ensure the strength and stability of the barrier that protects Altinna."

My heart sinks as I listen to them debate, their words echoing the fears that have been swirling in my mind since River showed up at my door this morning. They're so focused on the legalities, on what's allowed and what isn't, that they're missing the bigger picture. I can feel the power within me, the strength that both Akin and River bring out when they're near. But none of them seem to care about that. They're too caught up in the technicalities to see what truly matters.

"They're treating this like a legal dispute," River mutters beside me, his voice low and laced with frustration. "As if the laws could dictate something like this."

I glance at him, surprised to find that, for once, we're in agreement. The Council's discussion continues, growing more heated as they delve into the finer points of the law, wondering aloud if I'm even technically allowed to ascend the throne with more than one One. The longer they talk, the more my frustration builds. They're not getting to the point of how this could have happened, or what it means for the future of our kingdom. All they care about is the letter of the law, but I want answers about what this all means.

Finally, as the debate reaches a crescendo, Permiton, who has been sitting quietly until now, raises his hand. The voices slowly begin to recede as all eyes turn to him. He stands slowly, his expression thoughtful as he looks around the room.

"I've been studying the history of Altinna," he begins, his voice steady and measured. "Back to its founding, in fact. And I came across something that might shed some light on this situation."

There's a ripple of interest among the council members, and even my mother leans forward slightly, her eyes narrowing in focus.

Permiton continues, "The barrier that protects Altinna was first erected by a fae with silver eyes, just like Maerilee's. This fae was a powerful sorceress, and she was connected to not one, not two, but four different men. Each of them was her One, and together, they were able to create the barrier that has protected our kingdom for centuries."

A hush falls over the room as his words sink in. I feel a shiver run down my spine as I absorb what he's saying. Four Ones. The idea seems impossible, yet here I am, sitting beside two men who both strengthen my magic in ways I can't fully understand. Could it be true? Could I be meant to have more than one One, just like this ancient fae?

My mother is the first to break the silence.

"Permiton, are you certain of this? Do you have the text with you?"

Permiton nods, his expression serious. "I do. The book is in my study, but I can have it brought here immediately."

"Please do," my mother says, her voice firm. "This could change everything."

As Permiton sends for the book, the council members exchange looks, their earlier certainty now shaken. I can see the wheels turning in their minds as they try to reconcile this new information with the laws they've upheld for so long.

When the book arrives, it's an ancient tome, the leather cover worn and cracked with age. Permiton opens it carefully, flipping through the brittle pages until he finds the passage he's looking for. He reads aloud, his voice resonating through the room as he describes the fae with silver eyes and her four Ones. The council members listen intently, leaning forward to catch every word.

As Permiton finishes, he closes the book with a soft thud, the sound echoing in the silent chamber. The council members glance at one another, their expressions a mixture of awe and disbelief. It's clear that this revelation has thrown everything they thought they knew into question.

Finally, one of the council members speaks up, her voice hesitant but resolute.

"If the barrier was first erected by a fae who had four Ones, then it would only follow that Maerilee might be meant to do the same. This could be the key to strengthening the barrier, to ensuring that Altinna remains protected."

There's a murmur of agreement around the table, and I can feel a wave of relief wash over me. For the first time, it feels like we might be on the right path. The council members are no longer debating the legality of my situation. Instead, they're starting to see the potential, the power that this connection could bring to our kingdom.

My mother's expression softens as she looks at me, a hint of pride in her eyes.

"If this is true," she murmurs to me. "Maerilee, you have a great responsibility ahead of you. The strength of the barrier depends on you and your Ones."

I nod, my heart swelling with determination. I may not fully understand what's happening, but I know I'll do whatever it takes to protect Altinna. This is my duty, and I won't shy away from it.

Just as the pressure in the room begins to ease, Permiton speaks up again, his tone grave.

"There's one more thing we need to consider," he says, his eyes locking onto mine. "Maerilee, if you are meant to have four Ones, you're still missing two."

The room falls silent once more, the weight of his words hanging heavily in the air. My relief evaporates, replaced by a gnawing sense of unease. I hadn't even considered that possibility, that there might be more to this than just Akin and River. But if Permiton is right, if I'm truly meant to have four Ones, the matter is yet to be settled.

The council members begin murmuring again, their earlier relief turning back to concern. My mother's expression tightens, the worry returning to her eyes. She knows as well as I do that if I'm missing two Ones, it could mean that the barrier won't be fully strengthened until they're found. And who knows how long that could take? It's already taken this long to find the first two.

Akin reaches out, his hand finding mine beneath the table. His touch is warm and steady, grounding me in the midst of the uncertainty swirling around us. River, too, is watching me closely, his earlier frustration replaced by a look of interest that surprises me.

"We'll find them," Akin says quietly, his voice filled with quiet determination. "Whatever it takes, we'll find them."

I nod, squeezing his hand in return, though the unease remains.

My mother stands, her expression resolute as she addresses the council.

"We have much to consider, but for now, we must focus on ensuring the barrier remains strong. Maerilee and her Ones, however many there may be, will be the key to our kingdom's future."

The council members nod in agreement, and Mother adjourns the session. But the question lingers in the back of my mind: Where are the other two Ones? And what will it mean for Altinna if we don't find them in time?

CHAPTER 15
THIRD TIME'S THE CHARM

Maerilee

I leave the throne room in a daze, still processing what's just happened. I'm destined to strengthen the barrier, but that means I likely have four Ones. And here I've been worried that I don't have a One at all. It's all so overwhelming and hard to grasp.

On the one hand, I'm thrilled. The idea that I'm finally going to be able to do something to save Altinna, to protect our kingdom, is something I've longed for. But on the other hand, the reality of the situation is daunting.

River as one of my Ones? I think of my first impression of him when I saw him at the ball, his posture confident, his eyes glinting with his usual mix of arrogance and charm. I don't know how to feel about him in general. The connection between us is undeniable, of course. I can't pretend I didn't feel that surge of power when he kissed me. But the thought of being bound to him, of our lives being intertwined in such a significant way, fills me with uncertainty.

And then there's the matter of the other two. Two more men, somewhere out there, who are supposed to be part of this impossible equation. The thought makes my head spin. How am I supposed to find them? What if they're from a faraway kingdom, or in hiding, or worse? What if I can never find them at all? The weight of the responsibility feels like a mountain pressing down on my shoulders.

I can't stay in the antechamber any longer. Members of the Council are still milling around discussing, debating what all of this means for the future of Altinna. Right now, I just need to breathe. I need space to think. That's not going to happen here.

"Mother, Father," I say quietly, leaning toward them. "I need to excuse myself for a moment. I just need some time."

My mother looks at me with concern, but she nods, understanding in her eyes.

"Of course, Maerilee," she says. "Take all the time you need."

With a small, grateful smile, I make my way out of the throne room, then out of that wing of the castle altogether. The moment I do, the heavy atmosphere lifts slightly, and I take a deep breath, feeling a bit more grounded. I know where I need to go. The one place in the palace where I can always find some peace.

The library.

The corridors are quiet as I walk, my footsteps echoing softly against the stone floor. This part of the palace feels empty, almost too quiet, but it's a welcome change from the suffocating environment I just left. When I reach the library, I push open the heavy wooden doors and step inside, the familiar scent of old books and parchment wrapping around me like a comforting blanket.

I walk slowly between the towering shelves, running my fingers along the spines of the books, letting their presence calm my racing thoughts. This place has always been a sanctuary for me, a place where I can escape the pressures of court life and lose myself in the pages of history, of magic, of the world beyond these walls.

But today, I'm not here to escape. I'm here because I need answers.

I find a table near the back of the library, away from the doors, and settle into one of the plush chairs. For a moment, I just sit there, closing my eyes and letting the quiet wash over me. But the questions in my mind are relentless, and I know I won't find peace until I start looking through the stacks for some kind of solution.

I reach for one of the books on the table, a heavy tome bound in deep green leather with silver lettering on the cover. It's a book of magic, one that I've studied before, but never with the urgency I feel now. I flip it open, my eyes scanning the pages for any mention of the barrier, of the ancient fae who first created it, and of the Ones who were with her.

The words blur together at first, my mind still too scattered to focus. But as I force myself to slow down, to take it one sentence at a time, I begin to piece together fragments of information. The barrier was created by an extraordinary convergence of power, the magic of one fae amplified by her bond with four others. The connection between them was not just emotional, but deeply magical, their energies entwining to form a shield strong enough to protect an entire kingdom for millennia.

It's awe-inspiring, and it fills me with a sense of purpose. If I can find all of my Ones, if I can recreate that same bond, then I can strengthen the barrier against our enemies and save Altinna.

But the uncertainty remains. How am I supposed to find the other two? I have no idea where to even begin.

I'm so lost in my thoughts that I don't hear the door to the library open. It's not until I hear soft footsteps approaching that I look up and see Brook standing a few feet away, his expression hesitant but concerned.

"Maerilee," he says quietly, stopping a few steps from the table. "I didn't mean to disturb you. I just wanted to make sure you're all right. That was all very intense."

His presence surprises me, but it's not unwelcome. I give him a small smile, gesturing for him to sit.

"You're not disturbing me, Brook," I tell him. "Please, sit. I could use the company."

He hesitates for a moment, then takes a seat across from me, his gaze steady and gentle. There's a quietness about Brook that I find calming, and right now, I'm grateful for it.

"I was worried about you," he admits, his voice soft. "After everything that happened in the Council meeting, I thought you might need some time alone. But I also thought maybe you shouldn't be alone right now."

His words touch me, and I feel a warmth spread through my chest.

"Thank you, Brook, " I whisper, reaching out to squeeze his hand. "That means a lot to me."

There's a brief silence, and I can see that he's wrestling with something, his brow furrowing slightly. Finally, he speaks again, his tone careful.

"I know this is a difficult time for you, with everything that's happening," he says slowly. "And with River being one of your Ones…. I just wanted to say that I hope we can be friends."

His words catch me off guard, and I sense something of a sadness in him, as if friendship isn't really what he wants. Poor Brook always seems to be losing part of himself to his brother, always coming in second. Why couldn't Brook be one of my four, instead of River?

Then, a memory from the ball surfaces in my mind, an odd, fleeting connection I felt with Brook that night. It was nothing like what I felt with Akin or River, but it was there, a spark of something that I couldn't quite explain.

Before I can second-guess myself, I find the words slipping out.

"Brook, do you remember the ball? When we talked near the alcove?"

He nods, his expression curious.

"Yes, I remember."

I hesitate, feeling a flush rise to my cheeks, but I press on.

"I felt something when I was with you that night. I don't really know what it was or what it meant. I think maybe you felt it too."

Brook's eyes widen slightly in surprise, and I can see the emotions flickering across his face, uncertainty, curiosity, and something else I can't quite name. But then he gives a small nod, urging me to go on.

"Brook, can I kiss you?"

CHAPTER 16
SINCERELY YOURS

Brook

I can hardly believe what I'm hearing. For a moment, I just stand there, staring at Maerilee, waiting for the punchline. But the way she's looking at me, with those wide, earnest eyes, makes my stomach twist. This has to be a joke. It has to be. But why would she do that? Why would she play with me like this?

"You're making fun of me," I say, my voice hard and flat, even as my heart clenches painfully in my chest. "You're just like the others, aren't you? I should have known better."

The words taste bitter on my tongue, but I can't stop them. I can't bear the thought that she's like everyone else who has ever dismissed me, ignored me, or used me as the butt of some cruel joke. I turn on my heel, already halfway down the hall before I even realize I've started walking. My pulse is pounding in my ears, a mix of anger and hurt driving me forward.

How could I have been so stupid? How could I have let myself believe, even for a second, that Maerilee was different? That she saw something in me worth—

"Brook, wait!" Her voice is desperate, but I don't slow down. I can't. If I stop, I might just break.

But then, suddenly, her hand grips my arm, yanking me to a halt. I spin around, ready to tear myself away, but before I can say anything, her lips crash into mine.

It's like lightning strikes me, surging through my entire body. My first instinct is to pull back, to question what the hell is going on, but the power that floods me is too overwhelming, too real. It's unlike anything I've ever felt before, like the air is crackling around us, charged with something far beyond magic.

I can feel her in that kiss, really feel her. There's no joke here, no cruel twist. It's real, and it's powerful. The connection is undeniable, a bond that snaps into place with a force that takes my breath away. My hands instinctively find her waist, pulling her closer as I deepen the kiss, losing myself in the flood of energy coursing between us.

When we finally pull apart, we're both breathless. I search her face, looking for any sign that this isn't real, that it's all in my head. But all I see in her eyes is sincerity, a depth of emotion that mirrors what I'm feeling.

"I wasn't joking," she whispers, her voice steady. "I would never do that to you, Brook. I felt something that night at the ball, and I feel it even more now. I think you might be my Third."

Her words send a shockwave through me, and for a moment, all I can do is stare at her. My heart is pounding in my chest, my mind racing to catch up with what she's saying. Third. She thinks I'm her Third. It sounds insane, impossible even, but I can't deny what just happened between us.

Slowly, I raise my hand, feeling the power still thrumming under my skin, more potent than I've ever felt it before. I extend my fingers, focusing on the energy inside me, and with a simple thought, I unleash it.

The storm comes suddenly, dark clouds gathering outside the castle walls as thunder rumbles in the distance. The air grows thick with electricity, and I feel the rain pounding against the windows, the wind howling through the corridors. The castle itself seems to tremble under the force of it, and for a moment, I'm afraid I might lose control. But then I focus on Maerilee, on the connection between us, and I rein it in, letting the storm simmer just beneath the surface.

"I think you're right," I say, my voice barely audible over the fading storm. "But I don't know how this is supposed to work. Sharing you with River? With Akin? It doesn't make any sense."

I feel torn, my emotions swirling inside me. On the one hand, I'm overwhelmed by the connection we've just forged, by the sheer power of it. But on the other hand, the thought of sharing her, of having to watch her with my brother, with someone who has always overshadowed me, makes my stomach churn.

Maerilee takes a step closer, her hand reaching up to cup my cheek. The warmth of her touch soothes some of the turmoil inside me, but it doesn't erase the uncertainty.

"I don't know how it's going to work either," she admits, her eyes searching mine. "But I do know that I won't let this fracture you and River anymore. I promise I'll take care of any strife between you two. This is new for all of us, but we'll figure it out together. I'm not going to let you be pushed aside, Brook. You're just as important as the others."

Her words strike something deep within me, something that's been buried for a long time. The fear of being overlooked, of being the forgotten one, has always been a part of me. But Maerilee's promise, the way she looks at me like I matter just as much as anyone else is enough to ease some of that fear.

Still, the doubt lingers. River isn't just some other guy. He's my brother. And the thought of competing with him for Maerilee's attention, for her affection, is almost too much to bear. But when I look at her, when I feel the lingering power from our kiss, I know I can't walk away from this. From her.

I take a deep breath, my hand covering hers where it rests on my cheek.

"It's going to be hard, Maerilee," I say, my voice raw with emotion. "Sharing you with River... it's not going to be easy, to say the least. "

She nods, understanding in her eyes.

"I know it won't be easy, but we'll find a way. We have to."

I nod, though I'm not sure how any of this is going to work. But I know one thing for certain. I'm not going to let River or anyone else push me aside. Maerilee sees me, really sees me, and that's something I've longed for my entire life.

Maerilee

Brook seems to surge with a newfound confidence, and kisses me again, deeper this time. It's a kiss so passionate, I feel it down to my core. The air cracks with electricity around us as we back up, back into the library. Once inside, he pulls the door shut behind him, and I hear the sound of it locking.

My hands move to his shirt, quickly working the buttons until it hangs loose on his frame. This is crazy, I know that, but the power inside of me is pushing me to this. I need Brook, all of him, to feel whole. With Akin, it was slow, passionate, gentle. Now, I'm spurred on by an invisible force, desperate for Brook in a way I can't fathom.

I want to show him that he isn't second place to me. He is just as important to me as Akin, just as vital to my survival as River (though that's a thought I choose not to dwell on). All his life, he's been made to feel like he's less than, but that isn't true with me. Brook is special, and he should know it.

I sink to the ground, on my knees, and begin unbuckling his belt. I look up to him for permission, and he can only nod, swallowing hard as I unleash him from his trousers. He's stunning in my hands, hard and eager. I kiss the tip of his manhood before taking him in my mouth as far as he'll go. His hand tangles into the back of my head as his body relaxes against the door. When I look up again, his eyes are closed and he's lost in the sensation.

I suck, nip, tease until I can feel his entire body tensing. Just as I'm sure he's about to let go, he suddenly shouts for me to stop.

I meet his eyes in confusion, but there's a devilish look in them. For a moment, he looks so much like his brother, I could swear I'm being tricked. But there's a gentleness in his eyes that River simply doesn't possess, and my heart swells at the way he looks at me.

"When I come apart, I want to be inside of you," he says huskily, though the tinge of pink on his cheeks tells me that this isn't easy for him to admit.

A thrill of pleasure rips through my body and I nod, standing, and guiding him over to one of the overstuffed chairs. He sits at my command, a throne ready for me. I lift my skirt and climb on top of him, guiding him to my sex, nearly crying out in pleasure as I slide down his thick shaft.

I ride him hard, not wanting to be tentative with him. I don't want to leave any doubt in his mind that I want him any less than he wants me. His large hands grip my hips as I set a steady pace, rising up and falling back down onto him, feeling his large member stretch me wide. It's intoxicating.

I take him faster, deeper, more feral until I no longer feel like I'm tethered to the earth. He never lets go, though I can tell it takes concentration on his part. He lets me fall over the edge first, holding onto me as I come undone around him. I collapse on top of him as he continues thrusting into me until he finds his own release. As I rest in his arms, still straddling him, I lose myself in thought.

Just yesterday, I was convinced I might never find my One. Now, in the span of a single day, I've discovered three! It's dizzying, overwhelming, like the ground has shifted beneath my feet and I'm struggling to keep my balance. How is this possible? Has this always been my fate, or is there a reason, a purpose behind this sudden change of precedence?

As the thought settles in my mind, I can't help but think of

Direken's threats. He's planning something, something that could bring Altinna to its knees if we're not prepared. The barrier is weakening, and time is running out. Could this be Gaia's way of telling us we need to gather our forces? That we must act now, before it's too late?

It all feels so sudden, so urgent, as if the world is pushing me toward something I'm not fully prepared for. But I can't ignore the signs—the power I've felt with Akin, River, and now Brook. It's as if the pieces of a puzzle are falling into place, guiding me toward a path I never expected to walk. Whatever Gaia is trying to tell us, I can't afford to hesitate. We have to act, and we have to act now.

CHAPTER 17

YOU'VE GOT TO BE KIDDING ME

Maerilee

I walk back to the throne room with Brook by my side, his hand warm and steady in mine. The feel of his fingers intertwined with mine brings a strange mix of comfort and tension. Comfort, because despite everything, having him here feels right. But tension too, because I know what's waiting for us inside that room. More questions, more debates, and undoubtedly, more resistance.

As we approach the doors, I can already hear the raised voices, the overlapping arguments filling the air like a storm about to break. My stomach tightens, but I push it down, reminding myself of what I've just discovered. Brook is my Third. It's impossible, absurd even, but it's true. I can feel it in every fiber of my being.

I push open the doors, and the noise hits me like a wall. Many of the council members are still seated, deep in discussion, while my parents, River, and his parents are locked in their own heated debate. The moment we step into the room, all eyes turn to us. The sudden silence is almost deafening.

River's gaze falls to our joined hands, and his expression morphs into one of incredulity. He stares at us for a moment, his eyes flicking between me and Brook, before he lets out a disbelieving scoff.

"You've got to be kidding me!" he exclaims, his voice dripping with frustration, before he gets up and leaves the room.

I take a deep breath, steadying myself before I address my parents.

"Brook is my Third," I confirm, my voice firm despite the nervous flutter in my chest.

The words hang in the air, and I can see the shock ripple through the room. My mother's eyes widen slightly, while my father's expression hardens with concern. River's parents exchange looks of disbelief, their shock quickly turning into something sharper, more dangerous.

Brook squeezes my hand, grounding me, and I continue, my voice gaining strength.

"I have no idea who the Fourth may be, but I can sense that something is coming. We don't have much time. I need to find him, whoever he is, and soon."

The King of Oceana, River and Brook's father, steps forward, his face stern and disapproving.

"This is outrageous," he says, his voice cold. "We haven't even agreed to letting River get hand-fasted with this strange fae, much less both of our sons. This is not how things are done."

The queen nods in agreement, her eyes narrowing as she looks at me.

"There are protocols, traditions that must be followed," she agrees with sharpness in her voice. "We need to return to our king-dom, and you need to go through the proper courtship. You can't just claim both of our sons. It's unheard of. Maerilee will just have to pick one."

Her words strike me like a blow, but before I can respond, River comes back into the room, his eyes flashing with anger.

"No," he says, his voice cutting through the air like a knife. "There's no time for that. I agree with Maerilee. Something is coming, something big. We can't afford to waste time on formalities. This isn't about tradition. It's about survival."

His parents turn to him in shock, their faces a mixture of disbelief and outrage.

"River, you can't seriously be considering this," his father says, his tone laced with warning.

River's gaze hardens, and he meets his father's eyes without flinching.

"I'm not just considering it, Father. It's done. Brook and I are Maerilee's Second and Third. Whether you like it or not, this is how it's going to be."

The room falls into a stunned silence, and for a moment, all I can do is stare at River, my heart pounding in my chest. I never expected him to defend me like this, to stand up to his parents with such conviction. Despite everything, despite the complicated feelings between us, I feel a surge of gratitude toward him. He understands the urgency of the situation, and he's willing to put aside his pride and his past to stand by my side.

The Queen's face hardens, her lips pressing into a thin line.

"This is madness," she hisses. "You're throwing away everything we've built, everything we've taught you. For what? A fae who doesn't even know her own heart?"

Brook stiffens beside me, but I squeeze his hand, silently telling him to let me handle this. I take a step forward, meeting the Queen's glare head-on.

"This isn't about me not knowing my heart," I say, my voice steady and clear. "This is about the future of Altinna, about protecting all of our kingdoms. I didn't ask for this, but it's happening. We don't have time for courtships and formalities. We need to act now, before it's too late."

The queen looks like she wants to argue, but the king steps forward, his expression icy. "We're leaving," he says, his voice brooking no argument. "And our sons are coming with us."

Both River and Brook stiffen, their gazes locked on their parents.

The room feels cold, the atmosphere harsh, and everyone waits with bated breath to see what the two sons of Oceana will do.

"I'm staying," River says firmly, his eyes blazing with determination. "My place is here, with Maerilee."

Brook nods, his expression equally resolute.

"I'm staying too. We have a duty to Altinna, and I'm not going to walk away from that."

Their parents' faces darken with anger, and the Queen's eyes flash with fury.

"If you stay, you are betraying your own kingdom," she spits. "This is an act of war."

The words hang in the air like a dark cloud, and I feel the gravity of the situation settle heavily on my shoulders. This is more than just a family dispute now. This is about the fate of kingdoms, about alliances that have held for generations. But I can't let that sway me. The stakes are too high, and I know what I have to do.

I step forward, my voice calm but firm.

"There doesn't have to be a war," I say, meeting the Queen's glare with unwavering resolve. "We can still find a way to work together, to protect both of our kingdoms. But we need to move quickly. I need to find the Fourth, and we need to be ready for whatever is coming."

The queen scoffs, turning away from me in disgust.

"You expect us to believe that this isn't just some ploy to strengthen your own position? That you're not using my sons to secure your power?"

"No," I say, shaking my head. "This isn't about power. It's about survival. Threats have already been made against Altinna, and I have no doubt that they'll come to fruition. If we don't stand together, both of our kingdoms could fall."

The King's expression remains stony, but there's a flicker of doubt in his eyes. He glances at River, then at Brook, and finally back at me.

"If you truly believe this, then you must understand the consequences of your actions. If you fail, it won't just be your kingdom that suffers."

"I know," I say quietly. "And that's why we can't afford to fail."

There's a long, heavy silence as the king and queen exchange a look, the weight of their decision hanging over them like a shadow. Finally, the queen turns to her sons, her voice cold.

"If you stay, you will be cut off from our kingdom. You will no longer be our sons."

The words hit like a physical blow, and I see both River and Brook flinch. But they don't waver. They stand their ground, their expressions filled with resolve.

"We've made our choice," River says, his voice firm. "Our place is here."

Brook nods in agreement, his hand tightening around mine.

"We're staying."

The Queen's face contorts with rage, and she turns on her heel, marching toward the door. The king hesitates for a moment, his eyes lingering on his sons with something that looks almost like regret, but then he turns and follows his wife, leaving the room in a cold, tense silence.

As the doors close behind them, I let out a breath I didn't realize I was holding. The weight of the moment crashes over me, and for a second, I feel like I might collapse under the pressure of it all. But then I feel Brook's hand in mine, warm and steady, and I find my strength again.

"Thank you," I whisper, looking at River and Brook, my heart swelling with gratitude. "I couldn't do this without you."

River gives me a small, almost begrudging smile, but there's a hint of warmth in his eyes that wasn't there before.

"We're in this together," he says simply with a nonchalant shrug. As if this isn't the most important decision he's ever made in his life.

And for the first time since this whirlwind began, I feel a sense of hope. It's fragile, like a flicker of light in the darkness, but it's there. We may not have all the answers, and we may be facing impossible odds, but we're in this together. And together, we are strong.

CHAPTER 18

UNDER ATTACK

Maerilee

The moment the doors to the throne room close behind River and Brook's parents, the reality of the situation hits me like a tidal wave. War. Oceana has declared war on us. And with Direken already making threats, the danger to Altinna has never been more real. My heart pounds in my chest, the urgency of finding my Fourth crashing over me with the force of a thousand storms. I can't afford to wait any longer. Every second we waste brings us closer to disaster.

I turn to my parents, ready to discuss how we might find him, how we can gather the resources and magic needed to locate the last piece of this puzzle. But just as I open my mouth to speak, my mother's face pales, and she sways on her feet. The world seems to slow down as I watch her stagger, her hand reaching out as if to steady herself on an invisible support. My breath catches in my throat, and before I can react, she crumples to the floor.

"Mother!" I cry out, rushing to her side. My father is there in an instant, his face a mask of horror and fear as he kneels beside her. I grab her hand, feeling the coolness of her skin, the way her strength has suddenly drained away. Panic surges through me. This can't be happening. Not now. Not when we need her the most.

"Get the Healer!" my father orders, his voice tight with urgency, and one of the guards immediately dashes out of the room.

I cradle my mother's hand in mine, trying to hold back the tears that threaten to spill over. "Mother, please," I whisper, my voice trembling. "Stay with me. We need you."

Her eyes flutter open, but they're unfocused, her breathing shallow. It's as if something is sapping the life out of her, pulling her away from us. My father's hand trembles as he brushes her hair back from her forehead, his eyes filled with a fear I've never seen in him before.

The Healer arrives quickly, a small, older woman with sharp eyes and a no-nonsense demeanor. She drops to her knees beside my mother, her hands already glowing with the soft light of her healing magic as she begins to assess the situation.

"Is she going to be all right?" I ask, my voice barely more than a whisper.

The Healer doesn't answer immediately, her brow furrowed in concentration as she works. The glow around her hands intensifies, and I can feel the pulse of magic in the air, but it does nothing to ease the knot of fear tightening in my chest.

Finally, after what feels like an eternity, she pulls back, her expression grim.

"She's been poisoned," the Healer says quietly, looking up at me and my father. "It's a Parasitic Fae's work. The poison is sapping her strength, feeding off her life force."

My heart drops into my stomach, and a cold fury begins to build inside me. Parasitic Fae. That can only mean one thing. "Direken," I breathe, the name leaving my lips like a curse.

My father's eyes narrow, his hands clenching into fists.

It has to be him. The Oceanans are Water Fae, they wouldn't have the power to do this. But I didn't know much about Direken, other than that he gave me the creeps. With him being the only other threat to our kingdom, I have no doubt in my mind that he's behind all this.

The pieces begin falling into place as I consider all of the interactions I've witnessed between him and my mother. Direken has been planning this all along, weakening our defenses, poisoning my mother to ensure we're vulnerable when he makes his move. He's not just threatening war, he's starting it from the shadows, trying to dismantle us from within before we even have a chance to fight back.

"We need to seize him," I say, my voice firm as I look up at my father. "Before he can do any more damage."

But as the guards are called to capture Direken, another blow strikes.

"He's gone, Your Majesty," one of the guards reports, his face pale. "Direken has already left the castle."

A wave of frustration crashes over me, and I clench my fists, trying to suppress the fear gnawing at the edges of my resolve. Direken has slipped through our fingers, and now we're left vulnerable, our most powerful defender lying poisoned and weak. I glance down at my mother, her face pale and drawn, and the anger flares again, hot and fierce.

The Healer lays a gentle hand on my shoulder, her expression softening.

"She should recover within a week," she says, her voice reassuring. "But she must conserve her strength. She won't be able to use any of her power to keep the barrier up. She needs to focus on her health."

The implication of her words hits me like a blow to the chest. Without my mother's strength, the barrier that has protected Altinna for centuries will weaken even further. We're running out of time.

"Can't I try to strengthen the barrier?" I ask, desperation creeping into my voice as I look at my father. "I've already connected with three of my Ones. Maybe that's enough to—"

My father shakes his head, his eyes filled with sorrow.

"Maerilee, you would have to ascend the throne for the barrier to respond to you. Until then, it remains tied to your mother. Without her, it will continue to weaken."

The finality of his words leaves me breathless. The barrier won't respond to me unless I'm queen, and that can only happen if my mother steps down or . . . or if she doesn't survive this. The thought is unbearable, and I force it from my mind. I can't think like that. I can't lose her. Not now. Not ever.

But if I don't find my Fourth, if I don't gather all the strength I can muster, then Altinna could be lost, and everything my mother has fought to protect will be for nothing.

I look at Brook and River, both of them watching me with concern and determination. They're here with me, willing to stand by my side despite everything they've lost. Akin is standing a ways away, offering his quiet support the way he always has. And yet, even with them, I'm not enough. We're not enough. We need the Fourth, and we need him now.

"I have to find him," I whisper, more to myself than anyone else. But the words seem to echo in the room, heavy with the weight of our situation. "I don't know how, but I have to find him. It's the only way."

"Maerilee," Akin says softly, approaching me hesitantly. "There's nothing you can do right now. It's best to let your mother rest. You need it, too. This has been a trying day for all of us."

I look into his calming expression, and realize suddenly how difficult this must be for him. This morning, I was waking up in his arms, the two of us sure that we were it for each other. The world made some semblance of sense. Then, he learned that he had to share me with not one other man, but three. It truly has been a trying day.

Still, I feel restless and useless. The only thing I can possibly do to help is find the last man, my Fourth, and bring my powers to full strength. I owe it to my mother, to all of Altinna. I look between

Akin, Brook, River, and my father. All four men look at me with concern and a trace of pity.

My father turns his attention fully to Mother, though, and I tell my Three that I need a moment to myself. I can't think under the weight of their scrutiny. None of this is fair, and Direken needs to be brought to justice for trying to murder my mother.

I turn on my heel and storm out of the throne room for the final time, not caring what the Council or my Three think. The fate of Altinna rests on my shoulders. They can't possibly understand how difficult this feels.

CHAPTER 19
MAERILEE'S FOURTH

Maerilee

I pace back and forth in my room, my mind a whirlwind of anger and frustration. How could I have been so blind? I should have seen it. I *should* have known what Direken was doing to my mother. The signs were there. His unsettling presence at the ball, that strange, oily feeling that clung to him like a second skin. It all makes sense now, but it's too late. My mother lies poisoned, her strength sapped by his treachery, and I'm the one who let it happen.

I clench my fists, my nails digging into my palms as I replay the moments in my mind, searching for something I could have done differently. How could I have missed it? My mother's health has been deteriorating for days, and I just stood by, oblivious to the danger lurking right under our noses. I was so focused on finding my One that I didn't see what was happening right in front of me.

I should have been more vigilant. I should have protected her.

Anger courses through me, hot and furious, directed entirely at myself. I can't stop the torrent of self-recrimination that follows. I'm supposed to be the one to save Altinna, to strengthen the barrier and protect our kingdom. But how can I do that when I've already failed at the most basic task of all? I couldn't even keep my own mother safe.

Outside my door, I can hear the faint murmur of voices, the sound of my Three hovering just beyond the threshold. They're worried, I know. They've been trying to talk to me for the past hour, their voices a mix of concern and frustration as they plead with me to let them in, to let them help. But I can't face them right now. I can't bear to let them see how much I'm falling apart.

I stop pacing for a moment, my breath coming in harsh, uneven gasps. I press my hands to my face, trying to block out the world, to find some semblance of calm. But it's no use. The guilt gnaws at me, relentless and unyielding.

A knock sounds at the door, more insistent this time, breaking through the storm of my thoughts. I hesitate, hoping they'll go away, but the knock comes again, more forceful.

"Maerilee," a voice calls softly through the door. It's not one of my Three. It's Permiton.

For a moment, I'm tempted to ignore him too, to retreat further into my self-imposed isolation. But something in the tone of his voice, so calm and steady, yet urgent, makes me pause. I can't afford to shut everyone out. Not now, when so much is at stake.

I take a deep breath and cross the room to the door, my hand hovering over the handle for a moment before I finally pull it open. Permiton stands there, his expression serious but not unkind. There's a tension in his posture, a sense of purpose that makes me wary.

"Permiton," I say, my voice wavering slightly. "What are you doing here?"

He steps inside, closing the door behind him.

"I'm here," he says quietly, his eyes searching mine. "I wanted to see if there was anything I could do to help."

The kindness in his tone almost undoes me, and I have to bite down on my lip to keep the tears at bay.

"I don't know what to do," I admit, my voice breaking.

Permiton nods slowly, his expression thoughtful.

"I've been doing some research," he says, his voice measured. "There might be a way to help your mother, and by extension, the kingdom. But it's not without risk."

My heart leaps at his words, a flicker of hope igniting within me.

"What is it?" I ask, my voice urgent. "Tell me what I need to do."

He hesitates for a moment, as if weighing his next words carefully. Then, with a kind of resolve, he steps closer to me, his gaze steady. I expect him to say something, to tell me what he's found, but instead he takes a deep breath, and before I can react, leans in and presses his lips to mine.

He's stiff and awkward, more controlled and less passionate than any of my other connections. That describes Permiton, though, I think harshly. From what little I know of him, this is exactly how I would expect kissing him to feel.

The shock of the kiss holds me in place, my mind going blank for a split second. But then, just as quickly, I feel it, a surge of power, rushing through me like a river bursting its banks. It's a different kind of energy, a deep, ancient force that seems to resonate with something inside me, something I hadn't even realized was there.

Permiton pulls back, his expression tense, as if he's waiting for my reaction. My mind is reeling from the sudden rush of power, and for a moment, all I can do is stare at him, my heart pounding in my chest.

Permiton

When I kiss Maerilee, I feel my Sight unfurling, a wave of clarity washing over me as the images begin to form in my mind. I see Direken conferring with his army, setting a plan of attack. Then the army, dark and foreboding, marches steadily toward Altinna without any hesitation. They're massive, an endless wave of soldiers and twisted creatures, all moving with a single purpose. They want to destroy the kingdom where it stands. As they arrive at the border, the barrier gives them no resistance at all.

The barrier that has protected this kingdom for centuries is barely there, shredded and torn, weakened by Direken's attack on the queen. They walk through it as if it's nothing, as if it doesn't even exist.

My heart clenches at the sight, the weight of the impending devastation heavy on my chest. I have to tell Maerilee. She needs to know what's coming.

"Maerilee," I say, my voice low and urgent as I pull away from her. "I can See them. Direken's armies. They're advancing, and the barrier is barely holding. They're walking right through it."

She looks at me, her eyes wide with fear and determination, and I can see the weight of my words settle on her. But there's more. The image in my mind shifts, and I See the queen pouring the last of her strength into the failing barrier. She's fighting with everything she has, but it's killing her. The poison mixed with the strain of keeping up the border will kill her, and the kingdom will fall.

"And your mother," I continue, my voice tightening with the gravity of what I'm about to say. "She's still trying to save the barrier, even though it's killing her. She won't stop, Maerilee. Not unless someone stops her."

I can see the pain flash across Maerilee's face, the conflict tearing at her. She knows her mother would give her life to protect Altinna, but I can see she's not ready to lose her. Not like this.

I cast my Sight out further, reaching deeper into the threads of magic and fate that bind us all. And then, I see a flicker of something so powerful, so undeniable, that it makes my breath catch. The connection between Maerilee and the four of us brims with potential, but it's not fully realized. There's only one way to unleash it completely, to draw out the full extent of her power.

I clear my throat, feeling the weight of what I'm about to say, the sheer absurdity of it, but also the undeniable truth.

"Maerilee," I begin, my voice carefully measured. "I'm afraid you will need to have sex with every single one of us. To boost your power to its highest. And to maintain it."

The room falls into a heavy silence, the words hanging in the air between us. I can see the shock in her eyes, the way she's trying to process what I've just said. But I can also see the realization dawning on her, the understanding that this might be the only way. The connection we share isn't just emotional, it's deeply magical, and it requires a bond that's as physical as it is mystical.

"There's no other way," I add quietly, my gaze steady. "If we're going to save your mother, if we're going to save Altinna, we need to be at our strongest. All of us."

Maerilee takes a deep breath, the weight of the decision clear in her eyes. She's a queen in the making, but now, she's faced with a choice that could define the future of her kingdom. And she knows, as do I, that there's no time to hesitate.

CHAPTER 20
MIGHT AS WELL

Maerilee

The moment the words leave Permiton's mouth, I freeze. My mind scrambles to make sense of what he's just said, but all I feel is a surge of anger, hot and immediate. Did he really just suggest that? That I should, no, that I *must*, sleep with all of them? My hand moves before I can stop it, and the sharp crack of the slap echoes through the room.

Permiton doesn't react the way I expect him to. He doesn't flinch, doesn't show any sign of anger or surprise. Instead, he stands there, his expression unchanged, his eyes focused and unwavering.

That's when it hits me. He's not joking. He's not trying to make a move or disrespect me. He's dead serious. The only way that I can access the fullness of my powers is to be connected with all four of my Ones.

My anger dissipates as quickly as it came, replaced by a cold dread that settles deep in my gut. I shouldn't have done that. What an excellent impression I'm already making on him, and we've only been in each other's presence for a few minutes.

"Permiton," I start, my voice trembling slightly. "I'm... I'm sorry. I thought—"

He cuts me off with a small shake of his head.

"It's all right, Maerilee," he answers calmly, kindly. "I understand your reaction. I wouldn't suggest it if it weren't the best option. The only option, really."

I swallow hard, the weight of his words pressing down on me. This whole day has been a whirlwind of revelations, each one more overwhelming than the last. But as much as I want to deny it, to push it all away and pretend that things could somehow be different, I know deep down that Permiton is right. This is about more than just me. This is about saving my mother and saving Altinna.

And if this is what it takes....

I take a deep breath, trying to steady myself as I look at him.

"All right," I say, my voice firmer now. I might as well start with him. "We should get on with it then," I say rather awkwardly.

Permiton's eyes flicker with something. Surprise, perhaps, or maybe a brief moment of uncertainty. But he quickly nods, his expression settling into one of quiet determination.

"As you wish."

He kisses me again, though this time less stiff. He's still careful with me, his fingers barely ghosting over my face as if he's afraid I might break. It's him I'm worried about, but I let him guide me, let him lead me to the bed. His hands move to my hips, resting there as he kisses me gently, carefully.

He's thoughtful with every moment, stopping to ask me if I'm all right, if I'm okay with what he's doing. It's like he understands how difficult this is for me, how much stress I'm under to do everything correctly. Akin knows me better than anyone, and Brook is someone I feel the need to protect, but Permiton seems to really see me. Maybe that's his gift.

He undresses me slowly, purposefully, before laying me on the bed. I watch as he undresses himself, his movements sure and steady.

I take in his form, the breathtaking curve of his muscles. For an advisor, I must admit that he's very good looking and well-built. It must be from carrying all those heavy books. His eyes are dark as he watches me watching him. Soon, he's standing in front of me, completely laid bare. Yet it isn't just his body that's naked. He seems to be opening up to me in a way that I wouldn't expect from him. His vulnerability lies in his movements.

He slowly climbs on top of me, his own bare body just inches away. He kisses me deeply again, but not a single movement is wasted. This isn't about an all-consuming passion, it's about fulfilling a duty. Something about that makes me a little sad, but I cling to him as his fingers find my entrance, playing with me as I begin to open up to him.

I'm surprised by how well my body responds to him. He knows exactly where to touch to make me gasp, where to nibble on my neck to make me moan. Based on the kiss we'd shared, I couldn't have imagined that he would set me on fire the way he is now. Yet somehow, it feels completely calculated, like I'm a puzzle he's working out. He's just moving to each new piece to find what works.

He brings me to the brink of mind-bending pleasure before he finally enters me carefully, sliding inside of me as I scream out his name. As our lips connect again, I can't help but moan against his, feeling my pleasure wash over me as he thrusts into me at a steady pace.

We move together, and it feels almost surreal, like I'm outside of myself, watching this unfold from a distance. Yet as soon as he's inside of me, the magic between us flares to life, and I'm pulled back into the moment, into the reality of what we're doing. The connection is electrifying, just as it was before, but this time it's deeper, more intense. It's not just power, it's life, coursing through both of us, binding us together in a way that defies explanation.

The world narrows down to just the two of us, and everything else fades away. For a brief moment, there's nothing but the magic coursing between us.

I'm already chasing another round of pleasure, feeling the pressure in my abdomen begin to build. He is steady and constant, moving inside of me, then adding his fingers again when he realizes that I'm not quite as far along as he is. I gasp, unable to contain the surge of pleasure that washes over me as I once again fall over the edge at the same instant he comes undone inside of me.

When we finish, I'm left breathless, my body humming with the afterglow of power. I expect Permiton to say something, to offer some words of comfort or reassurance, but when I look at him, his eyes are unfocused, distant, as if he's looking at something I can't see.

"Permiton?" I ask, concern creeping into my voice as I sit up, pulling up the sheet to cover myself.

He blinks, his gaze sharpening as he comes back to the present. But instead of the tenderness I expect, his expression is tense, urgent. "I must go back to the library," he says, his voice flat, almost mechanical. "You must go see your mother. Now."

I'm taken aback by the sudden shift, by the way he seems almost disconnected from what just happened. "What? Why? What did you See?"

He shakes his head, already moving toward the door. "There's no time to explain. Just go. Your mother needs you."

Panic flares in my chest, and I scramble to gather my clothes, pulling them on as quickly as I can. Whatever Permiton has Seen, whatever has prompted this sudden urgency, I can't ignore it.

CHAPTER 21

ENEMIES ON ALL SIDES

Maerilee

I don't ask questions. I don't stop to think or even take a breath. The moment Permiton's words leave his mouth, I throw on a robe, my heart hammering in my chest, and run. The corridors blur around me as I race through the palace, my bare feet slapping against the cold stone floor. There's no time to waste. Something's wrong. Something's terribly wrong.

When I reach my mother's chambers, my pulse spikes. The door is ajar, a cold draft slipping through the crack as if beckoning me inside. I push it open, my breath catching in my throat at the sight before me.

She lies in her bed, deathly pale, her chest rising and falling with shallow, labored breaths. Her once radiant skin is ashen, and her eyes are closed as if she's already begun slipping away. I barely recognize her. She looks so fragile, so unlike the powerful woman I know so well.

I rush to her side, but her eyes are already closed, her body so still I fear I'm too late.

"No," I scream, shaking her gently. "No, no, no, you can't leave me!"

I cry against her cold skin, clutching her to me as I weep. I feel frantic, out of control, and I feel the sudden urge to fight. Maybe even to fight death. I will go to hell and back for my mother, I just need directions.

As I look up, something catches my eye. Beside her bed, a small vial sits on the nightstand, its contents dark and oily, the liquid swirling with an unnatural sheen. My stomach churns as I realize what it must be. Poison. My mother has been poisoned again!

I reach for it, my mind spinning, but a soft laugh stops me in my tracks. I whirl around, my heart pounding in my ears, and there, in the corner of the room, sits Eirliwyn.

He's draped casually in a chair, his legs crossed, watching my mother die with an unsettling calmness. His eyes flick up to meet mine, and for a moment, all I can feel is shock. I've known Eirliwyn my whole life. He's been one of my mother's most trusted advisors. How could he be sitting here, watching her die?

"You're too late, Maerilee," he says, his voice smooth, almost bored. "She's already beyond saving."

My hands curl into fists, trembling with a mix of fury and disbelief.

"What have you done?" I demand, my voice surprisingly steady as I stare him down.

Eirliwyn tilts his head, his lips curling into a bitter smile.

"Oh, Maerilee. Don't be so dramatic. This was inevitable." He gestures toward my mother's frail form. "She's held on to the throne for far too long. It's time for new leadership."

"New leadership?" I spit, my voice shaking with rage. "You've betrayed her. Betrayed us all!"

His eyes darken, and he rises slowly from his chair, stepping forward with a lazy grace. "Betrayed?" He lets out a short, humorless laugh. "No, Maerilee. This isn't betrayal. This is justice."

"Justice?" I repeat, disbelief coursing through me.

Eirliwyn's face hardens, and for the first time, I see the raw emotion simmering beneath his cold exterior.

"Your mother," he says, his voice low and venomous, "wasn't always so devoted to your father. We were in love once, she and I. She was mine. Until she discovered Fratino was her One." He spits the word like it's a curse. "She threw me aside like I was nothing."

I step back, my mind reeling. The bitterness in his voice cuts deep, but it doesn't change what he's done.

"You've poisoned her because she chose her One decades ago?" I demand, my voice trembling with disgust.

Eirliwyn steps closer, his eyes narrowing.

"This is about more than that, Maerilee. This is about power. I've waited centuries for this. I will be king, one way or another."

Before I can react, his form shifts, blurring at the edges as Shadow Magic envelops him. In an instant, he's no longer standing across the room, he's right next to me. His hand closes around my throat with a strength that takes my breath away. I gasp, my hands clawing at his wrist as I struggle to pull free, but his grip is iron.

"You will drink this," Eirliwyn hisses, his voice inches from my ear. His free hand lifts a vial, identical to the one beside my mother's bed, its contents swirling dark and malevolent. "And I will take what is rightfully mine."

I kick and thrash against him, panic rising in my chest. He's too strong, too fast, and I can't breathe. The edges of my vision blur, my strength fading as he forces the vial toward my lips.

The door bursts open.

Akin stands there, his face murderous. He charges into the room with a roar, his eyes wild with fury, and in one swift motion, he lunges at Eirliwyn. The force of the attack sends us all sprawling, Eirliwyn's grip loosening just enough for me to break free and stumble backward.

But Eirliwyn isn't so easily subdued. With a flick of his wrist, he vanishes again, disappearing into the shadows. Akin spins around, searching for him, but before he can react, Eirliwyn reappears on the other side of the room.

The vial slips from his hand as he vanishes again, and it shatters against the floor, the poison hissing as it dissolves into the air.

"No!" I scream, stumbling toward the shattered glass. "We need a sample of it! We need it for an antidote!"

River and Brook burst into the room, their faces grim as they assess the chaos unfolding around them. River moves quickly, trying to use his water magic to capture some of the poison, but it's too late. The dark liquid is already dissipating, vanishing into the air like smoke.

"Damn it!" River curses, slamming his fist against the floor.

Brook grabs a cloth and tries to soak up what remains, but the liquid evaporates too quickly. It's gone. All of it.

I turn back to my mother, my heart breaking as I rush to her side. She's barely breathing now, her skin cold to the touch, and I feel a sob rise in my throat.

"Mother, please," I whisper, grabbing her hand. "Please don't die. I need you. The kingdom needs you."

Her eyelids flutter, but there's no response. My mother, the strongest woman I've ever known, is slipping away, and I'm powerless to stop it.

Behind me, I hear Akin still struggling to locate Eirliwyn, his footsteps heavy as he moves through the room, searching the shadows.

"Where is he?" Akin growls. "I won't let him get away with this."

But Eirliwyn is always one step ahead. His form flickers in and out of the shadows, a blur of darkness that Akin can't pin down. And then, in a final burst of magic, Eirliwyn vanishes completely, his form dissolving into a cloud of smoke that rushes past us and out into the hall.

"Damn it!" Akin roars, following him out of the room to no avail.

The door swings open just as Eirliwyn escapes, and Permiton enters the room, his face a mask of calm focus. He pauses in the hallway, his eyes following the trail of smoke as it swirls past him. For a brief moment, I think he might be able to stop Eirliwyn, to catch him before he disappears entirely. But the smoke is gone before Permiton can act, vanishing into the air like it was never there.

Permiton turns to me, his expression grave.

"He's gone," he whispers into my ear.

I nod, my hands trembling as I cling to my mother's cold hand.

"He poisoned her, Permiton," I whisper, my voice broken. "I couldn't stop him."

Permiton pulls me against his chest in a move that surprises me. He holds me gently as I cry against him.

CHAPTER 22
THE NEXT RIGHT THING

Maerilee

I'm a broken shell of myself, held together only by Permiton's gentle embrace. My mother, still lying pale and motionless on the bed, is slipping away. Her chest rises and falls so faintly that, at times, I can barely tell if she's breathing. I squeeze her hand, willing her to hold on, to give me some sign that she can hear me, that she's still fighting. But there's nothing.

Someone sends for my father while the four of us wait in the room.

"Maerilee," Permiton says, his voice quiet but firm, drawing my attention away from my mother's lifeless form. His eyes are unfocused again, and I know he's seeing something beyond our reach. "The poison wasn't meant to kill her outright."

I frown, barely able to comprehend what he's saying.

"What do you mean?"

He takes a deep breath, meeting my gaze with a weight that makes my stomach churn.

"It's designed to keep her weak, ill, and unconscious. She could live like this for years, but she'll never wake up. She'll never be strong enough to rule, nor to strengthen the barrier."

The words hit me like a punch to the gut. My mother, my strong, capable mother, reduced to this, a living shell. And if what Permiton says is true, she'll remain like this forever.

"There has to be a way to save her," I whisper, more to myself than to him. "There has to be."

"There is," Permiton says, his voice steady. "But the antidote is the Bright Waters, located deep in the kingdom of Oceana, in the inaccessible part of the mountains. It won't be easy to find them. Many have tried and failed."

The Bright Waters. I've heard of them before, ancient and magical waters said to heal even the most deadly of wounds and poisons. But their location is rumored to be impossible to reach. Even if we had all the time in the world, it would be a nearly impossible task.

River steps forward, his jaw set in determination.

"Then we'll go," he says firmly. "We'll find the Bright Waters and bring back the antidote."

Brook, standing silently beside him, nods.

"We have to try," he adds, his voice soft but resolute. "For your mother, for Altinna."

Akin places a hand on my shoulder, his touch grounding me. At some point during my weeping, he's returned to his place by my side, exactly where he's always belonged.

"We'll all go, Maerilee," he says quietly. "We'll bring back the antidote. Whatever it takes."

I look at the three of them, their faces set with determination and loyalty, and a wave of gratitude washes over me. They're willing to risk everything to save my mother, to save Altinna. But the enormity of it looms over us all like a dark cloud. There's no guarantee they'll succeed. And every moment they're gone, Direken's armies draw closer.

As if reading my thoughts, Permiton's eyes glaze over, his Sight unfurling before him. He remains silent for a moment, his body still, as if he's seeing something far beyond the room we're in. Then, slowly, he blinks, his focus returning to the present.

"Altinna is no longer safe for any of us," he says, his voice grave. "Direken's armies are already marching toward the capital. They will be here soon, and the barrier is too weak to hold them back."

My heart sinks. I knew the barrier was weakening, but this is all happening too fast.

"Not to be the asshole here," River chimes in. "But if the queen dies, Maerilee can ascend the throne and strengthen the barrier. Maybe the best thing to do for the kingdom is to put her out of her misery. Respectfully."

Akin steps toward her, a mixture of pain and horror in his eyes.

"I should be the one to do it," he says mournfully. "I've served this family my entire life. I've sworn an oath to protect them, and if this is what it takes, it should be me."

He meets my gaze, and I see the tears forming in his eyes.

"I'm so sorry, Maerilee," he says, his voice breaking with sadness. "It's better that we end her suffering."

"No," I scream, scrambling to my feet. "I won't hear of this! She isn't gone yet, there has to be a way to save her. Right, Permiton?"

I look into his face to see it filled with sorrow. Whatever it is he's going to say, it isn't going to bring the comfort I so desperately need.

"Unfortunately, even if Maerilee were to ascend the throne, the barrier is too fragile," he warns us. "Maerilee, if your mother dies without the proper ceremonies of abdication, it will shatter. The transfer of power must be smooth, not forced. Otherwise, the barrier will be torn apart."

A heavy silence falls over the room. My chest tightens as the reality of the situation crashes over me. The only way for me to take over the barrier and save Altinna is if my mother abdicates properly. But she can't do that, not while she's trapped in this poisoned state.

The room is tense, the air thick with the weight of decisions that none of us are prepared to make. We're running out of time, and the options before us feel more and more impossible.

Permiton speaks again, his voice steady but filled with a quiet desperation.

"How do we know it won't work, though," River finally says, shattering the silence.

"Shut up, River," Brook spits at him. "You're not helping the situation. You just want to be the hero that saves the day, but there are no easy solutions here."

"Maerilee, what do you want to do?" Akin cuts in, his eyes focused on mine with a quiet strength.

"I don't know," I groan in frustration. "Permiton, walk us through the worst case scenario if she dies."

"If the queen dies without abdicating, the barrier will end. It will be as if we've ripped the very fabric of Altinna apart."

I clench my fists, frustration building inside me.

"So what do we do?" I demand, my voice breaking. "How do we stop Direken's armies if we can't even strengthen the barrier?"

The four men begin to bicker, each with their own opinion of how best to handle the situation. Permiton is ready with facts and figures, knocking down every solution that each one of them provides with practicality and laws. River is a bird trapped in a cage, desperately trying to fight his way out. He's a ball of nervous energy, eager to show that he's capable of taking charge, and growing increasingly frustrated with Permiton's wisdom.

Brook is doing his best to reign in River, while also proving that he's just as capable of coming up with a solution as his brother is. It's clear that he wants to help, but he's also trying so hard to be helpful.

Akin is in agony, both at the thought of losing my mother and the idea of Altinna falling to Direken's army. He keeps looking at me to gauge my reaction, checking that I am okay, but he's carrying his own burden of grief. Of the four men, he is closest to my mother, and losing her would destroy him.

Finally, Brook's voice breaks through the cacophony.

"Maerilee, this ultimately has to be your decision," he says gently. "You're next in line to rule. One way or another, you'll have to be the one to decide what happens next."

Before I can respond, the door swings open, and my father steps into the room, followed by my three siblings. His face is pale and drawn, his eyes filled with the same grief and fear I feel. He looks at my mother, lying still on the bed, and then at the rest of us, as if weighing the situation.

"Seal the room, Maerilee," he says, his voice calm but commanding. "Now."

CHAPTER 23

STRENGTH IN NUMBERS

Maerilee

"What do you mean by that?" I ask, my voice barely above a whisper, but my question hangs in the still air of my mother's chamber like a command.

My father stands at the foot of the bed, his gaze steady as it meets mine.

"You have enough power, Maerilee," he says, his voice low but certain. "You must. You wouldn't be where you are right now, wouldn't have found your Ones, if the power wasn't there. You can do this."

I blink, trying to process his words. I have power, yes. I can feel it, especially with Akin, River, and Brook close by. But enough to seal the entire room? To protect my family from whatever forces are marching on Altinna? The weight of his belief presses down on me, and I swallow hard, feeling the familiar thread of self-doubt pulling tight.

"I'm not sure if I can, " I confess, looking down at my hands as if the answer could be found in my own skin. "The most I've managed is a barrier around Duchess's ball. I'm not sure I'm powerful enough to protect you all."

I look ashamedly at my siblings, all gathered around Mother with matching expressions of grief and fear. It's my duty to protect them all, to keep them safe no matter what may befall us.

When I look up at Father, his expression hasn't changed. Despite everything, he remains calm, determined.

"You are stronger than you give yourself credit for, darling," he says with admiration. "I know you don't think you have what it takes, but I know that you can do this."

"If your family is safe here, we can go to Bright Waters," Akin whispers urgently into my ear. "We can save her, and save the kingdom."

"It's a good plan," Permiton agrees, and the others all seem to let out a sigh of relief.

"You are the only one who can do this," my father says, though his words don't assure me at all. "You can save us all."

Tears fill my eyes as I consider what I have to do. This will take all of the strength I have, and it still could fail. And that's all before I set off for a treacherous journey that will almost definitely fail. There's no good way to handle any of this, I know. But Mother needs me. The kingdom needs me.

"The best I can do is try, but my magic is still weak," I admit, feeling a sinking pit in my stomach.

Father approaches me slowly, his eyes filled with compassion. He lifts my chin up with his finger and looks into my eyes, filling me with a confidence I don't have in myself.

"Do what is necessary to make it stronger," he tells me kindly. "I know you can."

I break his gaze and look over at River, who's staring at me with a mix of interest and resignation. He's the last connection I have to make to access the full scope of my powers. I nod and tell my father that I'll be back as soon as I can. I lock eyes with River and motion for him to follow me as I leave the room, heading toward my own.

"You've saved the best for last, I see," he remarks cockily as we make our way down the hallway.

When we reach my bedroom, I turn on my heel, fixing him with a sharp gaze. I point my finger into his chest.

"Let's get one thing straight, you arrogant bastard," I snap. "You are the last man on this earth that I want to be linked to. You are rude and entitled. You treat others badly to make yourself look better. All you know how to do is make others feel bad."

His confident demeanor slips for just a second, but he throws it right back to me.

"And still, I'm your best hope of saving your kingdom, Princess," he snarls. "Don't forget, I defied my own parents and betrayed my nation for you. I stood by your side, even though I didn't have to."

"Would you like a prize for doing the bare minimum?" I screech at him. "We are bound to each other, you didn't have a choice."

"Of course I did!" he shouts, his voice echoing through the hall-way. "I didn't need to get myself tangled up in the politics of an infe-rior kingdom, but I chose to stay and be bound to you. Even though I have to share you, even though you're also bound to my much less worthy brother, I chose you. So get over yourself and let's do this."

He pushes open my bedroom door and storms in, his words catching me off guard. No matter how I feel about him, he has shown a loyalty to me that he didn't have to. He could have walked away.

"River, I'm sorry," I start as I follow him inside, but he turns on me, slamming the door shut behind me and pinning me against it.

"Don't be sorry, sweetheart," he growls with a smirk. "I like when we fight. It's kind of sexy."

I roll my eyes and bat at him, but he grabs my hand before I can hit him, and brings it to his lips. He kisses it softly, his eyes never leaving mine as his lips play at the sensitive spot on my wrist.

"There isn't time for this," I argue weakly, already distracted by the delicious things he's doing with his tongue.

"Oh, Maerilee," he grins. "There is always time for foreplay."

He kisses up my arm until he reaches the base of my neck, nibbling at the soft spot there. I gasp with pleasure, my fingers finding the base of his neck and clinging to his hair, keeping him there as he sucks on the tender skin.

"You have no idea how long I've wanted to do this," he whispers just below my ear, sending a shiver down my spine.

His hands move around me, finding the laces on my dress. He undoes them quickly, expertly, and my dress slips to the floor. His eyes darken as he looks at me, licking his lips as his eyes travel over my breasts, then lower.

"I want to fuck you against this door, Maerilee," he groans as his hands move to my hips. "I want to make you scream so loud they can hear you in Oceana."

He gives me no time to respond as his lips cover mine, his dominant and demanding. He's not gentle, but I can't help but admit that it turns me on. His hands move to my backside, squeezing and cupping until he lifts me up with one quick motion, leaving me breathless.

My legs instinctively wrap around his waist and I feel his hardness pressing into me.

"This is what you do to me, Princess," he growls against my skin. "You've been teasing me since the moment I arrived. I can't wait to be inside of you."

I moan as my head leans back against the door and I arch into him, my desire already evident. His pants are still on, but he makes quick work of that. He grips me tightly with one hand, while his other hand moves to unsheathe his member.

Foreplay is forgotten as he thrusts into me, his weight the only thing keeping me upright. He braces us against the door, his hand moving behind my head so that I don't hit the door as he relentlessly pounds into me. If I were of more present mind, I would be touched by the thoughtfulness of this action.

"Damn it, Princess," he moans as he continues his quick ministrations. "You're even better than I imagined you'd be."

"You imagined this?" I manage out, barely able to catch my breath as his thrusts cause a tight coil to form in the center of my stomach.

"So did you," he pants. "You might as well admit it now. You're stuck with me for life."

Something about his words drive me wild, the idea of having him like this forever intoxicating me. Though, to be fair, I don't know how long forever might last. There is so much at stake, so much contingent on me accessing my full powers.

Still, it can't hurt to enjoy the process, right? Waves of pleasure begin to course through me and I can't help but scream out River's name. Maybe he's right and they will hear me in Oceana, but I'm too far gone to care.

With a few final thrusts, he completely shatters me, and I cling to him as the waves of absolute ecstasy crash over me, causing me to nearly black out. I don't even notice as he walks us over to the bed and gently lays me down, holding me until I come back down to earth.

"Was that to your satisfaction, Princess?" he whispers into my ear, clearly pleased with himself.

"Shut up," I reprimand, slapping him on the arm. "We have work to do."

CHAPTER 24

THIS HAS TO WORK

Maerilee

As soon as River and I step into my mother's chamber, I'm struck by how still it is. My father stands near the bed, his hand resting gently on my mother's arm, while my three siblings, Jimmen, Orindan, and Carmelina, are gathered around the room, their faces pale and drawn with worry. The weight of the situation hangs in the air, thick and suffocating. My mother, once so vibrant, now looks so small, so fragile, lying there motionless.

I take a deep breath, trying to steady myself. I have to be strong. For her. For all of them.

"I'm going to try something," I say, my voice trembling slightly, but I force confidence into it. "I'm going to erect a barrier to keep you safe while we figure out how to save her."

My family watches me closely, their eyes filled with hope and fear. I can feel their expectation pressing down on me, and for a moment, the weight of it makes me falter. But I shake it off. I have to do this. I can't fail.

I focus on the magic within me, on the connection I've felt with Akin, River, Brook, and Permiton. It's there, simmering just beneath the surface, waiting for me to call it forth. I close my eyes and concentrate, pulling on that power, trying to form it into something solid, something protective.

For a moment, I can feel the barrier radiating from me. It flares to life around us, a shimmering field of energy that hums with power. But as soon as I let go of the focus, as soon as I stop actively concentrating on it, it flickers and disappears, vanishing into nothing.

I open my eyes, my chest tightening with frustration. I failed. Again.

"What am I doing wrong?" I murmur in panic, more to myself than anyone else. My hands clench into fists at my sides. I *know* the power is there, but it slips away like water through my fingers every time I try to hold it. Why can't I make it last?

Before I can spiral further into doubt, Permiton steps forward, his expression calm and knowing. He reaches out and takes my hand, his grip warm and steady.

"You're not doing anything wrong," he says softly. "Just remember, you don't have to do it alone."

I frown, confused.

"What do you mean?"

Permiton gives me a small, reassuring smile.

"You're trying to carry this burden by yourself, but that's not how this works. You don't have to do it alone, Maerilee. Let us help you."

He gestures to the others, and one by one, they step forward, each of them placing a hand on my shoulder, my elbow, my back. Their touch is grounding, steadying. I can feel their presence like a warm current, surrounding me, lending me their strength. Even Jimmen, Orindan, and Carmelina stand close, their eyes filled with silent support.

"Now," Permiton says, his voice low and even, "try again. But this time, draw on us. Let us lend our strength to yours."

I nod, taking a deep breath. I close my eyes once more and reach for the magic inside me. But this time, instead of trying to force it into place, I allow myself to feel the connection to the others. It's like a thread running through all of us, binding us together, and as I pull on it, the power that flows through me multiplies, growing stronger, more focused.

Suddenly, it's as if a floodgate opens. I'm no longer just accessing my own magic. I can feel Permiton's Sight, the way he perceives the world in layers of possibility and energy. I can sense the moisture in the air, the subtle shift in the atmosphere, every droplet vibrating with its own life force. I'm acutely aware of my body, of the tension in my muscles and how to command them with precision. There's a wealth of power at my fingertips, more than I've ever felt before.

But with that power comes a sense of danger. It's overwhelming, like standing at the edge of a cliff, knowing that one wrong step could send me spiraling into the void. I can feel the magic swirling inside me, wild and untamed, and for a moment, I'm terrified that I'll lose control, that I'll hurt the people I love.

I can't let that happen.

But as the panic rises within me, I feel the others. Their presence anchors me, keeps me grounded. Akin's steady hand on my shoulder, River's unyielding grip on my arm, Brook's gentle touch at my back. They remind me that I'm not alone. I'm not standing at the edge of this power by myself. They're here, holding me steady, keeping me from falling.

I let out a shaky breath, my fear ebbing as I focus on them. They're not just lending me their strength, they're helping me stay in control.

With that realization, I push aside my worry for my mother. I know it's there, lingering at the edges of my mind, but I can't afford to let it distract me. Not now. Not when so much is at stake. I can't let her down. I can't let any of them down.

I concentrate on the barrier again, pulling the magic around us, shaping it into something solid, something protective. I can feel it forming, stronger this time, more stable. It hums in the air around us, a shield of shimmering energy that pulses with the combined power of all of us.

But as soon as I try to release it, to let it stand on its own, it flickers again. My concentration wavers, and the barrier falters, dissolving before my eyes.

Frustration flares in my chest, and I grit my teeth, my hands shaking with the effort of holding the magic in place. I try again, focusing harder, but the same thing happens. The barrier slips away, fading as soon as I loosen my grip on it.

"I can't," I mutter, my voice thick with frustration. "It's not working."

But the others don't let go. They stay with me, their hands steady on my skin, their magic flowing into me like a constant, unwavering current.

"You can," Akin says softly, his voice calm and sure. "Don't stop. We're with you."

I take a deep breath, my heart pounding in my chest. I want to believe him, but the failure stings. The weight of it presses down on me, making it harder to breathe.

But I can't stop. I *won't* stop. Not until I've done everything I can.

I close my eyes again, letting the power rise within me, feeling the steady pulse of it as it weaves through me, through all of us. I let the fear slip away, focusing only on the magic, on the way it moves and breathes inside me.

Slowly, carefully, I form the barrier again, drawing it tighter around us, making it stronger, more focused. I don't release it this time. I hold it in place, feeling it solidify with every heartbeat.

I can sense the anxiety in the room, the fear and hope that everyone is holding onto. My father, standing so still by my mother's side, watching me with that quiet strength he's always had. My siblings, holding their breath, waiting for something to change. Akin, River, Brook, and Permiton all beside me, their presence like a lifeline, their belief in me unwavering.

I can't fail them.

The barrier flickers again, but this time, I don't let it go. I grip the magic tighter, forcing it to hold, willing it to stay solid. My muscles burn with the effort, and I can feel the strain of it pulling at the edges of my consciousness, but I refuse to let go.

And then, suddenly, it clicks into place.

The barrier hums around us, a steady, unyielding shield of magic that glows faintly in the air. It's not perfect. It wavers at the edges, fragile in places, but it's there. It's holding.

I open my eyes, breathless, and look around the room. Everyone is watching me, their faces filled with a mixture of relief and awe.

"You did it," Permiton says softly, his voice filled with quiet pride.

I let out a shaky breath, the tension in my chest loosening just a little.

"I did," I whisper, though I can hardly believe it myself.

But there's no time to celebrate. My mother still lies on the bed, her life slipping away with every passing moment. And this barrier, no matter how strong, won't hold forever.

I turn to the others, my voice steady but urgent.

"Now we need to find the Bright Waters. We don't have much time."

They all nod, their faces set with determination. We've made it this far, but the hardest part is still ahead, and we're running out of time.

CHAPTER 25

IMPOSSIBLE GOODBYES

Maerilee

I close my eyes, focusing on the magic coursing through my veins. The power is there, simmering beneath the surface, waiting for me to command it. I can feel the barrier beginning to take shape in my mind, a protective shell around this room, around my mother and family. But this time, I need more. It needs to be specific, targeted, able to allow some things in and keep others out. Food, water, air, those must pass through. But nothing else. Nothing that could harm them.

The magic resists at first, slipping through my grasp like water. But I don't give up. I take a deep breath, reaching deeper, pulling on the strength I know I have inside me. And not just my own strength, Akin's, River's, Brook's, and even Permiton's. Their magic intertwines with mine, amplifying it, making me stronger. With their power, I push through the resistance.

Suddenly, I feel it solidify and obey.

The barrier flares to life around us, invisible but undeniably there. It hums with energy, a quiet pulse that tells me it's working. I open my eyes, breathless and light-headed, and look around the room. My family is still here, watching me anxiously, but the air feels different now. Safer.

My entire body feels like it's been wrung dry. I'm completely drained. I lean against the wall, sliding down until I'm sitting on the floor, trying to catch my breath. The magic took more out of me than I expected. But it's done. We're safe. For now.

As I sit there, letting the weariness wash over me, a thought creeps into my mind, unbidden and unwelcome. If this took so much out of me, just to set a barrier around a single room, how did the First Fae manage to erect a barrier around the entire kingdom? And how can I ever be expected to strengthen that barrier?

The enormity of it staggers me. The sheer amount of power it must have taken to protect all of Altinna is beyond anything I can imagine. And yet, it was done. For generations, the barrier has held, protecting us all. But now, as it weakens, as it threatens to fall apart completely, I wonder if I'll ever be able to restore it? If the barrier goes down while I'm gone, will I be able to raise it again?

The thought tightens in my chest, sending a wave of doubt crashing over me. What if I'm not strong enough? What if, after everything, I fail?

"Maerilee," Permiton's voice pulls me from my spiraling thoughts. He's kneeling beside me, his hand resting lightly on my arm. His eyes are calm, reassuring, and when I look into them, I can see the depth of his confidence in me. It steadies me, grounds me.

"Don't worry about the future," he says softly, his voice like a soothing balm to my frayed nerves. "Focus on the now. Focus on getting the Bright Waters. That's what matters. Everything else can wait."

I nod, though the doubts still linger at the edges of my mind. But Permiton is right. I can't afford to worry about what might happen. Right now, I need to focus on the task at hand. We need to save my mother. We need to get the Bright Waters, and that's all that matters.

With a deep breath, I push myself to my feet.

"We should get going," I say, trying to shake off the exhaustion. "The barrier will hold while we're gone."

Akin steps forward, his eyes filled with quiet concern.

"Are you sure you're ready?" he asks quietly. "We can wait for you to get your strength back."

I nod, even though I don't feel ready at all. There's no time to rest. Every second we waste brings us closer to losing my mother, closer to losing Altinna.

"We don't have a choice," I say, my voice steadier now. "We need to move quickly."

River, always practical, nods in agreement.

"Then let's pack up and go. We'll need supplies for the journey."

Together, we begin preparing for the trip to Oceana. I hug my family tightly before I leave the safety of the room. We all must go to our own chambers to pack our things. Akin will pack the additional supplies like food and camping gear, while River and Brook go to gather maps of Oceana.

In the silence of my room, I can't help but think about the journey that awaits us. Oceana is far, and the path to the Bright Waters is treacherous, especially now, with Direken's armies on the move. But I know we have to try. For my mother. For Altinna.

I pack light, only the essentials. I grab a few changes of clothes and some small vials of healing potions the Healer left for emergencies. But as I look at the supplies, I wonder if it will be enough. We don't know how long the journey will take, or what we'll encounter along the way.

Several minutes later, we meet back at the door of my mother's room, so I can say one final farewell to my family. My men give me space as I hug each of my siblings tightly, filled with the responsibility that I must save our mother.

. . .

WHEN I GET to my father, his eyes are full of unshed tears, though he's beaming at me with pride. He pulls me into his arms and squeezes tightly, pressing a quick kiss to the top of my head.

"Don't forget that you are stronger than you think," he whispers into my hair. "You have all the power you need, you just need to believe in yourself enough to access it. You can achieve everything you wish, and more."

I swallow hard and nod, wiping away my own tears. It's impossible to leave him like this, not knowing if I'll return. And if I don't return, what will happen to him? What will happen to my siblings, who look to me for strength and guidance? What will happen to my mother?

When we're ready to go, the five of us gather at the door. I glance around the room one last time, my gaze lingering on my mother's still form. The barrier hums faintly in the background, a reminder of the magic holding this space together, protecting her, protecting all of us. I wish I could do more. I wish I could stay here and make sure she's safe, but I know that's not possible.

"We'll be back soon, Mother," I whisper softly, though I know she can't hear me. "Just hold on."

My father, standing by the bed, gives me a small nod of encouragement. His eyes are heavy with worry, but there's a quiet strength in his posture. He believes in me. He believes in us. And I have to believe in myself, too.

I turn to the others, my heart pounding in my chest.

"Let's go."

We step out of the room, and I close the door behind us, sealing it with the barrier one last time. The magic thrums in the air, steady and strong, and I know it will hold while we're gone. At least, I hope it will.

The palace is eerily quiet as we make our way through the corridors, the weight of the situation pressing down on all of us. The silence only serves to heighten my awareness of the task ahead, the dangers, the uncertainties, the impossible odds. But with each step, my resolve strengthens. This is what I have to do. I have no other choice.

As we step outside, the cool air of the evening wraps around us, carrying with it the faint scent of rain. The sky above is dark and clouded, the stars hidden behind a blanket of shadow. It feels like the whole world is holding its breath, waiting for something to break.

River takes the lead, his gaze focused on the horizon.

"Oceana is a long way," he says quietly, "but we'll make it."

Brook nods, his expression serious.

"We don't have time to waste. If we push hard, we can make it in a few days."

Akin falls into step beside me, his presence solid and reassuring.

"We'll get there," he says, his voice steady. "We'll find the Bright Waters and save your mother. All will be well."

I nod at Akin's words, though the knot of anxiety in my chest doesn't ease. The road ahead is long and perilous, and even with the best of intentions, there's no telling what we'll face. But his steady presence beside me, along with River's sharp focus and Brook's quiet resolve, gives me the strength to keep moving. Permiton is quiet, though that isn't unusual. He seems to be lost in his own visions, searching the future for our possible outcomes.

We move in silence through the darkened streets of the capital, heading toward the stables where fresh horses await us. The night feels heavy, as if the air itself is pressing down on us, reminding me of the urgency of our mission. Direken's armies are out there, moving closer with every passing hour. And my mother, still lying in that bed, her life hanging by a thread, depends on us finding the Bright Waters in time.

As we reach the stables, the stable hands greet us with hushed voices, sensing the gravity of our departure. The horses are saddled and ready, their breaths visible in the cool night air. I place a hand on the neck of the mare in front of me, letting her steady warmth calm my racing heart.

"Let's move quickly," Permiton says, his voice cutting through the stillness. "We'll ride hard through the night. The faster we reach Oceana, the better."

The rest of us nod in agreement, and soon we're mounting the horses, preparing for the long ride ahead. My fingers tighten around the reins, and I cast one last glance back toward the palace, my mind lingering on the barrier I've left behind. It's still strong, still holding. But for how long?

Permiton rides up beside me, his expression unreadable in the dim light.

"Don't doubt yourself, Maerilee," he says quietly, his voice barely above a whisper. "The barrier will hold as long as it needs to."

I bite my lip, unsure if I should share my deepest fears with him. But before I can respond, River calls out, "Let's ride!" and we're off.

THANK YOU FOR READING! Find Book 2, *The Quest, here.*

ALSO BY SADIE WATERS

Chosen by the Princess: A Reverse Harem Romance,

Realm of the Chosen Book 1

Loved by the Princess: A Reverse Harem Romance,

Realm of the Chosen Book 2

Ruled by the Princess: A Reverse Harem Romance,

Realm of the Chosen Book 3

Realm of the Chosen: The Complete Series

Demon Seer: Ember's Flames Book 1

Demon Hunter: Ember's Flames Book 2

Demon Slayer: Ember's Flames Book 3

Queen of Winter

A Sketch Away from Perfect: The Art of Having it All Book 1

A Palette Full of Lovers: The Art of Having it All Book 2

Book Three coming soon!

The One: Four Fae for the Princess Book 1

The Quest: Four Fae for the Princess Book 2

The Crown: Four Fae for the Princess Book 3

Follow me on social media!

Instagram: https://www.instagram.com/sadiewaters/

Facebook: https://www.facebook.com/sadiewatersauthor

Twitter: https://twitter.com/SadieWatersBook

Bookbub: https://www.bookbub.com/authors/sadie-waters